"Katha, you should have taken a break. Let me massage these muscles," Vince said, placing his hands on her shoulders.

Gently, he ordered himself. She was so delicate, he needed to be careful.

Katha sighed. "Oh, that feels marvelous," she murmured, eyes half-closed. He had such strong hands, but he was tempering his strength with gentleness, just as he had when he'd held and kissed her. The heat from his hands was swirling lower, making her whole body ache and yearn for more. "I'll get back to work now," she said.

"No, relax a bit."

"But . . ." She turned to look up at him. She hadn't realized they'd be this close, so close. She wanted to slide her hands up his chest, feel the taut muscles beneath. She wanted to nestle her body to his, to invite his kiss with her lips. "Vince, I—"

His fingers tightened as he looked directly into her smoky green eyes. Eyes that radiated the same message of desire as his did. Move away from her, his mind demanded.

Not a chance, his heart answered.

"Katha," he murmured with a groan that seemed to come from his soul. He lowered his head and kissed her, swept away by the tide of passion that had been building within them for so long. . . .

WHAT ARE *LOVESWEPT* ROMANCES?

They are stories of true romance and touching emotion. We believe those two very important ingredients are constants in our highly sensual and very believable stories in the *LOVESWEPT* line. Our goal is to give you, the reader, stories of consistently high quality that may sometimes make you laugh, sometimes make you cry, but are always fresh and creative and contain many delightful surprises within their pages.

Most romance fans read an enormous number of books. Those they truly love, they keep. Others may be traded with friends and soon forgotten. We hope that each *LOVESWEPT* romance will be a treasure—a "keeper." We will always try to publish

LOVE STORIES YOU'LL NEVER FORGET
BY AUTHORS YOU'LL ALWAYS REMEMBER

The Editors

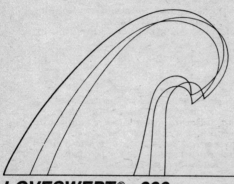

LOVESWEPT® • 386

Joan Elliott Pickart
Mixed Signals

BANTAM BOOKS
NEW YORK • TORONTO • LONDON • SYDNEY • AUCKLAND

MIXED SIGNALS

A Bantam Book / March 1990

*If you would be interested in receiving protective vinyl
covers for your Loveswept books, please write to this address
for information:*

*Loveswept
Bantam Books
P.O. Box 985
Hicksville, NY 11802*

ISBN 0-553-44018-7

Published simultaneously in the United States and Canada

Bantam Books are published by Bantam Books, a division
of Bantam Doubleday Dell Publishing Group, Inc. Its trademark, consisting of the words "Bantam Books" and the
portrayal of a rooster, is Registered in U.S. Patent and
Trademark Office and in other countries. Marca Registrada.
Bantam Books, 666 Fifth Avenue, New York, New York 10103.

PRINTED IN THE UNITED STATES OF AMERICA

OPM   0 9 8 7 6 5 4 3 2 1

For
Boots and Debbie
and
Anita and Ray

One

"Lieutenant Santini, what are your plans now that you've resigned from the police force?"

"No comment. Let me through, please."

"Lieutenant, over six months ago you returned from Italy after participating in the Exchange-a-Cop program. Do you think you might go back to Italy?"

"No comment," Vince Santini repeated. He continued to move down the wide, brightly lit corridor of city hall, his progress slowed by the throng of reporters. "Don't you people have anything better to do? Cops leave the force all the time. This isn't big news."

"*You're* big news," a woman said. "You were chosen for that program in Italy; you've solved a remarkable percentage of your cases; you've been bucking the system and city hall since day one and getting away with it. Now you quit. Why? And what are your plans for the future?"

Vince shook his head, frowning. "No comment."

"Come on, Lieutenant," a man said, "give us a break."

"I have nothing to say."

Vince pushed open the door and left the building. The reporters scrambled to keep up with his long-legged stride as he strode down the concrete stairs to the sidewalk.

The November Los Angeles sky was overcast, and the chilly, dull gray day did nothing to improve Vince's rapidly deteriorating mood.

Obviously, Vince thought, there had been a leak in the department, the reporters tipped to the fact that Lieutenant of Detectives Vincent Santini was meeting with the commissioner that afternoon to turn in his official resignation.

Still, Vince would never have anticipated being descended upon by the press corps. If he could just get away from these clowns, they'd forget who he was within an hour. Granted, for several years his name had been in the paper countless times with regard to cases he'd been involved in solving. But to reporters, a retired cop was a boring cop, and if he could make his escape, he'd be out-of-sight, out-of-mind.

"Lieutenant, you were in Army Intelligence before

you joined the police force. Any chance you'll work in one of the government's special agencies now?"

"No comment." Vince paused at the bottom of the stairs. He had no desire to lead the group to where his car was parked around the corner. "Look," he said, facing the group, "I'm not trying to be hard to get along with. I just don't have anything to say. I'm going to take a vacation for a couple of weeks, relax, think things through, consider my options."

"Vacation. Where are you headed?"

Vince shook his head. "You're not giving me an inch. You're leaving me no choice but to say, 'No comment.' Now, move out of my way. I've had enough of—"

The screeching of tires interrupted him, and all heads snapped around to look toward the curb. A bright red compact car had been brought to an abrupt halt in front of city hall. Leaving the car engine still running, a young woman flung open the door and ran toward the group gathered on the sidewalk.

Her full-speed-ahead approach caused the startled reporters to part their ranks like the Red Sea. She launched herself at Vince, flinging her body against his, her arms wrapping around his neck.

Vince staggered slightly at the unexpected impact, then instinctively held on to the feminine bundle plastered against him.

"Darling!" the woman said, loudly enough for all to hear. "I'm just so dreadfully sorry I'm late picking you up. Forgive me?"

She batted her eyelashes at him in an exaggerated manner, ending in a very decisive wink.

Vince was unable to stop the smile that curved his mouth. The woman's green eyes were sparkling with mischief and merriment. Short, curly auburn hair surrounded a very pretty face, that included a dusting of freckles across a pert nose, and soft, tantalizing lips.

He did not have the foggiest idea who this delectable woman was, or why she'd thrown herself at him. What he did know was that small, firm breasts covered by a pale green T-shirt were pressed tightly against him, and her slender jean-clad legs were nestled to his own. He was also aware that his libido was rapidly becoming disturbed by their intimate embrace.

"I forgive you," he said, still smiling at her.

"Oh, good," she said sweetly. "Then let's be on our way, shall we, darling? I'm sure these lovely people will excuse us. We'll just hop into my little car and off we'll go. Okay?"

She was rescuing him from the reporters, he thought incredulously. Unless she was a reporter herself, one who possessed more of an imagination than the others. If that was the case, he'd deal with it later. For the moment . . .

"We're out of here," he said. He grabbed her hand and started toward the red car. "See ya," he called over his shoulder to the astonished group on the sidewalk.

"I'll drive," the woman said to Vince. "My car is temperamental."

"Fine," he said.

He had barely managed to fold his six-foot-three-inch frame into the passenger seat and close the door when the car shot forward. He grabbed the dashboard and took a closer look at his chauffeur.

Whoever she was, she was an attractive woman in a down-to-earth, wholesome way. She also drove like a maniac, and it would be a miracle if she didn't wrap the little red car around a telephone pole.

"You could slow down a bit," he said. "It's not as though we robbed a bank, you know. Those reporters couldn't possibly have gotten to their cars in time to be following us."

"Oh." She nodded and let up on the gas pedal a fraction of an inch. "There."

Vince rolled his eyes, then looked at her again. "I hate to get personal, but who are you? And why did you rescue me from the press?"

"Hang on," she said, and zipped through a yellow light.

"Where are the cops when you need them?" he muttered.

"Cute," she said, and slumped back in the seat. Oh, good grief, Katha Logan thought, what had she done? She'd scooped Vince Santini up off the sidewalk and hauled him away, that's what she'd done.

She had seen his picture in the paper a couple of times, but that hadn't prepared her for the real thing. He was incredible—tall and well-built, his skin olive-toned, his hair and eyes as dark as coal.

He had long, muscular legs and wide shoulders, and his features were rough-hewn, masculine, and absolutely gorgeous. In tight, faded jeans and a light blue dress shirt, the man was a modern-day Roman god. And she'd kidnapped him! Well, no, not exactly kidnapped. After all, he'd been more than happy to come along . . .

"Hello?" he said. "Before I meet my Maker because you drove us into the side of a building, could I at least know who you are?"

"Oh, sure. I'm Katha Logan." She gave him a quick smile, then redirected her attention to the traffic.

"Katha Logan," he repeated. "Katha. Unusual name, and I like it. So, Katha Logan, what's this all about?"

"I need your help. I came downtown to see you and heard you were over at city hall, resigning. I must say, your timing is awful. I've read so much about you in the papers, and a friend of mine said you'd been in charge of solving a series of liquor store holdups a while back—her father owned one of the stores, you see—and you caught those guys in a matter of days. That clinched it for me. I knew you were the one to handle this."

She inhaled a gulp of air.

"But you resigned just when I needed you. Drat. Anyway, then I decided that you might at least offer an opinion about this mess, even if you weren't on the police force anymore. Why did you quit? Never mind. It's none of my business. So, when I got to city hall and saw the reporters mob you, I knew I'd never get near you. I went for my car, came to the front of the building and, as they say, the rest is history." She took a deep breath as she ran out of air. "Get it?"

Vince nodded slowly. "Yes, I think I actually understood all of that. I assume you're having some kind of trouble that requires a detective. I'm not a police officer any longer, Miss Logan."

"Oh, call me Katha, and I'll call you Vince. Okay? I realize you're no longer a detective, Vince, but you didn't turn in your brain with your gun and badge. Couldn't you just hear me out? Give me your opinion?" She frowned. "Oh, dear, that won't work."

"Why not?"

"Because you're not being paid by my taxes now. Anything you do in the way of an investigation would come under the heading of private eye, I guess, and those guys charge a bundle." She sighed. "Well, so much for that plan. Where would you like me to drop you off? Oh, I imagine you'd prefer to go back for your car, wouldn't you?"

"Whoa," he said, raising one hand. "It's too soon to go back to city hall. I'm sure those reporters are still hanging around."

Actually, the press would be long gone, and Vince knew it. He just didn't want to be dropped off yet, never to see the enchanting, albeit somewhat nutty, Katha Logan again. She was as refreshing as a breath of spring air. Not his type, of course, but intriguing nonetheless.

He could listen to her story, then recommend someone on the force who could help her. He owed her that much for rescuing him from the reporters.

"Look," he said, "why don't we have a cup of coffee in that café up ahead. The circulation in my legs is being cut off from the way I'm folded up in here."

"All right."

Vince closed his eyes as Katha cut across two lanes of traffic to pull into the parking lot of the café. She slammed on the brakes, and he let out a pent-up breath.

"We're here," she said.

"We're alive," he muttered. "That's the really amazing part." He opened the door and eased his way out of the car.

Inside the café they ordered coffee and danish, then Vince leaned back in the booth and folded his arms loosely across his chest.

"You have the floor, Katha Logan," he said. "I'm all ears."

Not quite, she thought dryly. He was all man, every delicious inch of him. She'd had a brief glimpse of what it was like to be held in Vince's strong arms when she'd flung herself at him in front of city hall. Ecstasy, that's what it had been. He'd felt so good, so powerful. For that moment, she'd been vitally aware of her own femininity, and felt safe and protected in the embrace of a very masculine man.

He must have women flocking after him in droves, she mused. Sophisticated women with fancy clothes and long, manicured fingernails.

Blondes. Yes, he probably went for tall, voluptuous blondes, who would look dynamite on his arm. Vince Santini was most definitely out of her league. And this train of thought was thoroughly depressing her. She had enough problems without sighing wistfully over a man who wouldn't look twice at her.

"Katha?"

"Oh, yes. I'm sorry. I was daydreaming for a minute there." She sat up straight, lifted her chin, and met his gaze directly. "I run a business called Logan and Logan Typing Service which—"

"Excuse me," he said, raising one hand. "There are two of you Logans?" Her husband? he wondered. She wasn't wearing any rings, but that didn't mean she wasn't married. The other Logan probably was her husband.

"Yes, two Logans," Katha said. "Me and—" She stopped speaking as the waitress placed their coffee and danish in front of them.

And? Vince mentally prompted, then berated himself. What difference did it make who the other Logan was?

"My father," Katha said, when the waitress moved away.

Before he even realized it was there, a smile broke out across Vince's face. "Oh, your father. You're in business with your father. That's nice. I mean, go ahead with your story."

"No, there's really no point in it," she said. "You're no longer a detective. Well, your *brain* is, but *you're* not, and I can't afford your brain."

"Don't worry about that. If I have the facts I might be able to connect you with the right person in the right department."

"Oh, I see," Katha said thoughtfully. "Well, all right, here goes. I work out of my house. My father's house, actually. My clients are mostly students from the colleges in the L.A. area, along with a few small businesses. They type their material, usually rather haphazardly, onto a computer disk, then send it to me over a modem. It's printed out in that rough form, then I retype it in finished format and deliver it to them by messenger. There are a lot of people who just don't type well, and I provide a much needed service."

He nodded. "Clever. I do a two finger hunt-and-peck method of typing myself. My college papers were not prize specimens."

"Our reputation for error-free material is spreading, and we're getting more business all the time. I have a secretary, but when term papers are due at the colleges, I have to hire an extra typist to keep up with the work load. The password to patch into my modem is posted at schools and businesses. The client can code in and place his name on the schedule for a specific time to transmit his work. It all goes amazingly smoothly once they get the hang of it. The colleges have computer labs with the equipment the students need to send their material to me."

Vince polished off his danish, drained his coffee cup, and nodded. "Okay, I get the picture. So, what's the problem?"

Katha glanced around, then leaned toward him. Her voice was low when she spoke. "Vince, a message came over my modem yesterday that wasn't meant for me. It was a glitch, a transmission mistake. It was suddenly just there in my printout basket."

"And?"

She opened her purse and took out a folded piece of paper, which she spread out in front of him. She looked quickly around the room again, then tapped the paper with one finger.

"Read that," she said.

Vince noted the troubled expression on her face, then directed his attention to the paper.

" 'Virus in place to switch welfare rolls at end of month,' " he read aloud quietly. " 'Be ready to replace addresses before first.' " He met Katha's gaze. "I sure hope you know what this means. It's gibberish to me."

"I do know what it means. In computer jargon a virus, sometimes called a rogue, is a code hidden in a software program that gives a specific command at a predetermined time. The virus is illegal, has been planted by someone who managed to break into the program undetected. It's very high-tech crime."

"I'm following you," he said. "Go on."

"This message says that a virus is in place to change the welfare address rolls, which means there will be no checks delivered to those people. It instructs the other party to plant a new, phony address list at exactly the proper time. The checks will be sent to those addresses, I imagine, and cashed before the real recipients can report not receiving theirs. It's a one-shot operation that will net the criminals an unbelievable amount of money."

Vince stared at her, at the message, then back to her. This was crazy, he thought. How could someone pull off a scam like this? It seemed inconceivable, ridiculous. Yet he remembered a news story a year or so ago about a college kid who managed to foul up several thousand government computers with a mischievously placed virus. The amount of planning that would have to go into the sort of crime Katha was suggesting was daunting, but if someone really knew his computers . . .

"You don't believe me, do you?" she said softly.

He blinked, focusing on her, on her lovely face with its guileless, sincere expression. His logical police training was telling him to be very skeptical, yet looking at Katha, he knew he'd never forgive himself if he walked away from her right then.

He started to speak, but she interrupted.

"Vince, you've got to believe me. The welfare system in this city is going to come to a screeching halt in two weeks if that virus isn't found. People are going to go hungry, be unable to pay their rent, their day-care costs . . . The list just goes on and on."

"But we know the virus is there." Assuming, he added silently, she was right about that message.

"Don't you see? The program to print the addresses can't be run on schedule unless the virus is found. Otherwise, the program will be totally erased. Even if they started this very minute typing in the names and addresses on a fresh program, they'd never finish in time to get those checks out by the first."

"How would they replace the real addresses with the phony ones?"

"Apparently they have the password to the master system. The original address list is erased, the phony one slides into place. The source of the transmission is heaven only knows where. The checks and envelopes are printed with new addresses and off they go. No one is going to notice anything wrong because it's a procedure done month after month."

He shook his head. "Unbelievable." But he was starting to believe it.

"I hardly slept a wink last night, going over and over this in my mind. Viruses are extremely difficult, but not impossible, to find in a program. It takes long hours of tedious work, but it can be done. The thing is, the crooks will just hightail it out of town when they realize their plan was stopped. They'll go to another big city and start over. They have to be caught, Vince."

"Hey," he said, covering one of her hands with his, "take it easy. You're really getting upset." He stroked her wrist with his thumb. Such a small hand she had, he thought. Delicate, with skin as soft as a rose petal. Katha Logan cared deeply about people. Her distress over the welfare recipients whose checks might be in jeopardy was genuine. "I assume you told your father about this."

"No," she said, slipping her hand from beneath his, "I didn't tell my father. He's . . . Well, I didn't. You're the only one who knows."

"The message inadvertently came over your modem. Would you say they've figured out that it went to the wrong place?"

"Maybe, but not necessarily. If there's a power dip, a message can be lost completely and has to be sent again. They were careless to transmit something like this over a modem. They're obviously well trained in computers, but their judgment isn't the best."

"Which would work to their disadvantage. I must say, Katha Logan, you seem to have stumbled onto a real can of worms here."

"Does that mean you believe me? I was hoping that you . . . Well, at least you can tell me who I should talk to in the police department."

Vince turned his head to look out the window, his eyes narrowed in concentration.

Katha's concern about the virus faded as she studied his profile. His features seemed to have been chiseled from stone, his straight nose, high cheekbones, square jaw. He was magnificent.

"Vince?"

He turned to look at her.

"I shouldn't have snatched you up off the sidewalk the way I did. This must be a difficult day for you. I don't imagine your decision to quit the police force was an easy one to make."

"No, it wasn't, but it was a long time coming, and was overdue. I'm not burned out on police work. It was the politics that got to me, the red tape, the fifteen rules for the simplest procedure. I wasn't answering the reporters' questions because I don't like being pushed to the wall like that. The truth of the matter is, I know exactly what my plans are. I'm opening my own detective agency. As of right now, Katha Logan, you are my first client. How does that sound?"

"No, no. I can't do that because I couldn't afford to pay you. Besides, the welfare computer program isn't mine, it belongs to the city. I just happen to be aware of the danger the system is in."

"True, but think about this. If we turn this over to the police and there's one leak in information, there goes any chance of catching these guys."

"What are you suggesting?"

"That I poke around a bit on my own, see what I can dig up, before we decide when to go to the police." He grinned at her. "It'll be good practice for me to see what kind of private detective I'm going to make. No charge. This is on the house. What do you say?"

"It sounds reasonable, except for one tiny change I have to make in your plan."

"Which is?"

"*We*, as partners, will poke around a bit. *We* will see what *we* can dig up. I'm involved in this through no fault of my own, Vince Santini, and I intend to follow it through to its proper end. Besides, you need my computer experience. So? Are we partners?"

He looked at her for a long moment, then a slow smile crept onto his face. "Miss Logan, *we're* going to be virtually inseparable."

A shiver danced through Katha as she saw the disconcerting gleam in Vince's dark eyes.

Oh, good grief, she thought, for the second time that day, what had she done?

Two

At midnight that night, Vince flung back the blankets on his bed. Naked, he strode across the room to the large window. The drapes were open, affording him a spectacular view of the city lights that seemed to stretch into infinity. From his vantage point of twenty floors up, he could see the cars along the roadways, the vehicles appearing like ants marching in formation.

He braced one hand high on the window frame and ran the other over the back of his neck, hoping to ease the tight muscles. His inability to relax, to shut off his mind and sleep, disgusted him. He was only too aware he was losing the mental battle against the unsettling events of the day.

And for the first time in many years, he felt absolutely and chillingly alone.

"Dammit," he muttered, shaking his head.

The decision to quit the police force had been a long time in coming. Frustration and anger had been building within him at the ever-increasing rules, regulations, and politics that had halted his progress at every turn, hindering his investigations. He'd had to leave before he blew a mental fuse and destroyed a fine career and reputation.

But now, in the silence of the night, the decision weighed heavily on his mind and soul. He envisioned himself as a ship afloat in a large, empty sea with no goal, nor another human being, in sight.

Foolishness, he admonished himself. He'd carefully planned the next door he'd walk through before closing the other behind him. His application for a private investigator's license had been approved, and the laminated identification card was tucked securely in his wallet. His gun permit and the weapon it allowed him to carry were in his nightstand drawer. He was officially a private detective.

His restlessness that night, he reasoned, was understandable. His life was undergoing some monumental changes. But why the feeling of loneliness that was like a cold fist in his gut? Why the sense that there was something missing from his existence that a new and challenging career could not provide?

Vince turned from the window with another muttered expletive. Crazy, he told himself. He, was getting punchy, from lack of sleep. There he stood wide awake while Katha Logan probably slept as peacefully as a baby.

Katha Logan.

He went back to bed and stretched out, his hands linked beneath his head as he stared up at nothing. The image of Katha filled his mind's eye.

Pretty, wholesome Katha, he mused, with her fluffy auburn curls, big green eyes, and dusting of freckles on her nose. Katha, who had leapt into his arms and felt custom-made just for him. Katha, his partner, in his first investigation as a private detective.

Sleep crept over him. Lovely . . . lovely . . . Katha.

Katha sat bolt upright in bed, as wide awake as though someone had shaken her. She glanced at the clock, saw that it was twelve-twenty-eight, and blinked several times in confusion.

Why was she awake? Had she heard something? No, all was quiet, but she'd been jolted awake as if it were morning instead of just after midnight. How very strange.

She eased back against the pillow and folded her hands on her stomach. So, go back to sleep, she told herself. She had too much to do to be groggy the next day. Sensible people were asleep. Vince Santini was probably asleep.

Vince Santini.

What a man, she thought, smiling. She was not an expert on men, but even she knew when she was looking at, gazing at . . . well, okay, *gawking* at, an incredible specimen of the male species. He was something, all right. Big and strong, dark and beautiful. When he touched her, smiled at her, spoke to her in his deep, rich voice, she melted like butter in the sun.

Starting tomorrow, though, she'd quit acting like such a ninny around him. She was his partner in a vitally important investigation, not a Santini groupie. Yes, tomorrow she'd shape up her act.

But tonight? Tonight was hers, and it was brimming over with delicious thoughts and images of Vincent.

Vince . . . She yawned as sleep drifted over her. Vince Santini . . .

At one o'clock the next afternoon, Katha slid into the booth across from Vince and smiled at him. She told herself that her heart was beating rapidly because she'd run the length of the restaurant parking lot, and that the funny flutter in her stomach was from hunger.

But seeing Vince's handsome face, his warm smile, she knew she was lying to herself. Three seconds in the man's presence and she was all in a dither. This would never do. Well, if everything else failed, fake it.

He would never know he was pushing her sensual buttons.

"Hi," she said brightly. "I'm sorry I'm late. I had to wait for the messenger to pick up some typing, then the traffic was grim, and . . . But here I am, ready to go to work, partner."

"You're not that late," he said, signaling to the waitress. "Let's order our lunch."

"You bet. Whatever trips your trigger, Lieutenant."

"What?" he asked, with a burst of laughter.

"That's cop jargon. I saw it on television. I'm not a complete novice when it comes to police work, you know."

"That's comforting," he said, still chuckling. "What do you want to eat, Ace?"

They ordered hamburgers, fries, and chocolate milkshakes, then Vince studied Katha as she spread her napkin on her lap.

She looked sensational in her sunny yellow sweater and dark slacks, he decided, and he'd caught a glimpse of her slender legs and nice bottom as she'd zoomed into the booth. Her cheeks were flushed and her eyes were like emeralds. When she smiled, her whole face lit up—and heat churned low in his body.

She was so . . . real. Yes, that was the word. He had the sudden urge to haul her across the table and into his arms, then kiss her until neither of them could breathe. *That* would most definitely trip his trigger.

"So," she said, jolting him from his wayward

thoughts, "where do we start? What's first on the agenda?"

"Slow down, Katha. I think I'd better make something very clear. You're going to stay in the background in an advisory capacity. You're the computer expert. I'll do the investigating and come to you with any questions I have. How's that?"

She leaned toward him and narrowed her eyes. "That stinks. This is my crime, Vince Santini. I found it, and we're partners in solving it. You're not going to have all the fun of skulking around in the shadows while I sit on the shelf. That's simply not fair." She sat back and nodded decisively.

Vince stared up at the ceiling for a moment, then met her gaze. "In the first place, Miss Logan, no one said anything about skulking in the shadows."

"Well, of course you skulk. All police types skulk. I saw it on—"

"Television. So you mentioned. Cops spend more time filling out reports in triplicate than skulking. And in the second place, I don't want you visibly active in this. This isn't a small operation, you know. We're talking about a heist that involves a great deal of money, and these people aren't going to take kindly to any attempt to stop them. If the police force was investigating, the crooks would probably take off if they heard any rumors that interest was being paid to the welfare department. In my case, if they have someone on the inside tipping them off, they'll figure that one man isn't much of a threat."

"I swear, " she said, teasing, "you've got that cop jargon down pat. Small operation, someone on the inside . . . Awesome."

He laughed. "Just pay attention, will you?" She really was like a breath of fresh air, he thought. Absolutely delightful. "Time out. Here comes our lunch."

She smiled. "Somehow you're blowing your image having a chocolate milkshake. Big, tough cops are supposed to drink coffee . . . black."

"I do," he said, matching her smile, "when there's no way to get a chocolate milkshake." He realized he'd smiled and actually laughed aloud more in the past ten minutes than he probably had in the previous two weeks. Katha's vivacious personality was infectious. That was fine, as long as he didn't forget that he was supposed to be concentrating on a serious situation. "Eat up, Katha."

They ate in silence for several minutes, then Katha asked, "Do you have any family, Vince?"

"Where did that come from?" he asked. "I thought you were all wrapped up in this potential crime."

"I'm not sure," she said seriously, "that discussing such a thing while eating is good for one's digestion. Therefore, do you have any family?"

"Cops don't stop talking about their cases while they eat, or nothing would ever get solved, but we'll do this your way. No. I don't have any family."

"None?"

"No. My parents were killed in a freeway accident

when I was seven, and my grandfather raised me. He died ten years ago."

"And you've never married?"

"Never. I don't believe that police work is conducive even to a serious relationship, let alone marriage. The odds for divorce are too high. I made my choice on that subject many years ago, and as a private detective I'll feel the same way."

"Oh."

"Oh? That's it? Most people take my stand on the issue as the signal to launch into a debate."

"Everyone has a right to his own opinions and choices," she said, with a little shrug. "You never intend to marry. End of story." And that was *not* a flicker of disappointment that danced around her heart. "May I have the ketchup, please?"

He handed her the bottle. "What about you? Logan and Logan is you and your father. Are there more of you Logans here and there?"

"No, just the two of us. My mother died four years ago. I had already graduated from college and started my own business. It was Logan Typing Service then, and I ran it from my apartment."

"And now you've teamed up with your father, and you're living in his house?"

"Yes. My father . . . Well, it's better this way."

Why? Vince wondered. "Is there a special man in your life?" Not that he cared, of course. He was just making idle conversation because it wasn't good for one's digestion to discuss police work while one was eating. "You know, a man who thinks along the lines of marriage, babies, mortgages."

"I was engaged to a man I met in college. We were going to marry after he got his master's degree in math. But when I moved home to my father's house, he . . ." She paused. "Well, it didn't work out. I really haven't had time for a serious relationship because . . . because I've been very busy expanding Logan and Logan."

"I see," Vince said, but he really didn't. There was something missing, something she wasn't telling him. Her eyes had lost their sparkle too. Lord, her eyes were expressive. She'd better not ever play poker. "I . . . um, would guess you'd like to marry someday, have some kids."

She looked at him for a long moment. "Yes," she said quietly, "maybe someday."

He frowned at her pensive tone, and they finished their meal in silence. When the waitress cleared their plates, he asked for a cup of coffee . . . black. Katha said she couldn't eat another bite.

"Question," he said after the coffee had been set down in front of him. "This glitch, as you called it, that caused that message to come over your modem was a fluke, right?"

"Yes, I assume so. They'd have no reason to intentionally send the message to me."

"What are the chances of it happening again?"

"I have no idea."

He nodded. "It's worth checking out. Are you free for a couple of hours?"

"Yes. My secretary is at the house working on what needs to go out this afternoon. I'm ready to concentrate on our crime."

Her eyes were sparkling again, he thought. "Then, let's do it. Oh, and *I'll* drive."

Their destination, much to Katha's amazement, was a huge luxury yacht docked in the marina of an exclusive country club.

As they boarded the yacht, they were hailed by a tall, well-built man in his early thirties.

He was, Katha decided, very handsome, with his sun-streaked light brown hair, deep tan, and ready smile. But not as good-looking as Vince, nor quite as well-built, nor were his eyes—brown with flecks of amber—as compelling as Vince's nearly black ones. He was a captivating man in his tight jeans and fisherman's sweater, but even he couldn't match the potent aura of masculinity emanating from Vince.

"How in the hell are you, Vince?" the man said, shaking Vince's hand and whopping him on the shoulder. "It's great to see you."

"Katha Logan," Vince said, "meet Tander Ellis."

"Hello," Katha said, smiling.

"Welcome aboard, pretty lady," Tander said. "You make these humble and somewhat tacky surroundings glow with your mere presence."

"Ignore him, Katha," Vince said, chuckling. "He's so full of blarney and bull, it's a sin. Tander, control yourself. Katha came with me, she leaves with me."

"Oh?" Tander said.

"Yeah," Vince said. "Got that?"

"Yes, sir, mighty Lieutenant," Tander said. "You're breaking my fragile heart, of course, but it wouldn't be the first time you've cut me off at the knees. If you say Katha is your lady, Vince, then that's how it is. No problem."

"Oh, but . . ." Katha started.

"Good," Vince said.

Well, for heaven's sake, she thought. She felt like a bone being haggled over. But she also felt very feminine and pretty. Vince's lady? That wasn't true, of course, but it had a lovely sound to it. No, forget it. Just forget it.

"So, Vince," Tander said, "I read in the paper that you copped out of the cops. Didn't surprise me, you rebel. I've been amazed that you lasted as long as you did in the establishment. So, what's the plan? Are you finally going to live in the manner the inheritance from your grandfather could make you accustomed to?"

Katha looked quickly at Vince. Inheritance? Was Tander Ellis insinuating that Vince was wealthy?

"No," Vince said. "That money is in the hands of my investment broker."

"Boring," Tander said. "I had hopes for you when

you bought that penthouse apartment, but you went right on playing cops and robbers."

"And I still am. I'm a private detective now."

Tander shook his hand. "I'm giving up on you. Katha, for such a beautiful woman, you have lousy taste in men. Now, I know how to enjoy myself and the millions available to me. Sail away with me, my princess, to exotic lands."

"I can't today," she said, laughing. "I have a thousand things to do."

"Well, damn."

"Tander," Vince said, "I need to pick your pea brain a bit. Katha and I are working on a case that she brought to me."

"Big?"

"Big."

"Then let's go below and get comfortable. That wind off the water is chilly." Tander rubbed his hands together in anticipation. "Big, huh? And no establishment rules to follow? Santini, you're just what I need to break the boredom of the idle rich."

Katha gasped when she saw the magnificent room below that Tander led them to. Royal blue and gold were the prominent colors, and the wood was dark, gleaming mahogany. The chairs and sofas were upholstered in leather, and thick blue carpeting muffled their footsteps. Both Katha and Vince declined Tander's offer of refreshments, then Katha settled in the center of a sofa.

Tander started toward her, received a glare from

Vince, then laughed and shook his head as he raised both hands in a gesture of peace.

"Okay, okay. I was just double-checking, that's all." He slouched into an enormous armchair. "Katha is yours. I get it, I get it."

There they went again, Katha thought, sighing inwardly. Anyone observing all of this would conclude that Katha Logan was the exclusive property of Vincent Santini.

She watched as he shrugged out of his gray windbreaker. No, she didn't belong to him. He wanted no part of a serious relationship. Even if he did, she wasn't his type, nor did she play the sort of games she imagined he was used to. She must not pay one bit of attention to the curling warmth within her that was caused by Vince's this-woman-is-mine act.

He turned to lay his jacket over the back of a chair, and her eyes widened as she saw the gun nestled in the back of his belt.

Looking up, he caught her surprised expression. "Habit," he said. "I automatically carry a gun, Katha. It wasn't necessary today."

"I can remember a few times in the old days that I was very glad you had it," Tander said. "You pulled us out of a tight spot or two, Vince."

"You did the same for me."

"Were you a police officer, Tander?" Katha asked.

"Me? Lord, no. Vince and I did some wild and wooly things in funny, foreign places for the Feds many years ago. That was in our reckless youth. As many times as we came close to buying the farm, I still have fond memories of that nonsense. Our problem was, we actually believed that we were indestructible. Yet it turned out that we were."

Vince chuckled and sat down next to Katha, stretching one arm along the top of the sofa behind her.

Well! she thought indignantly. There were a dozen places he could have sat, but he plunked himself down right next to her. She could feel his heat; smell the light aroma of his musky after-shave; see his well-defined thigh muscles beneath the soft material of his jeans. Darn the man. He was carrying this game too far.

She cleared her throat loudly. "You two have certainly had some fascinating adventures, it would seem. However, I think it's time we concentrated on the business at hand."

"Yes, ma'am," Vince said solemnly. She shot him a dark look. "Here're the details, Tander."

Forgetting nothing, Vince gave Tander an accounting of what had taken place.

"Is what you quoted me the exact wording of the transmission that came over Katha's modem?" Tander asked.

"Yes," Katha said. She opened her purse and removed the paper. "Would you like to see it?"

Tander crossed the room to take the paper. A frown knit his tawny brows together as he paced back and forth, reading and rereading the message.

Katha watched him prowl and decided he reminded her of a caged lion with his sun-streaked hair and taut, muscular body. She sensed a leashed strength in him, like the power she felt in Vince. Despite Tander's devil-may-care facade, he had an intensity just as potent as Vince's.

"What's your problem, Ellis?" Vince finally asked. "You've read the thing at least a dozen times. Facts are facts. Someone's setting up the welfare department to rip off a lot of people who can't afford it. I want them."

Tander stopped his pacing and faced Vince. "Dammit, Santini," he said, dragging one hand through his wind-tousled hair, "I've never known you to go off half-cocked. You're jumping in with both feet, not knowing how deep the water is."

Vince narrowed his eyes. "What in the hell are you talking about? Can't you read what's in front of your eyes? Katha explained to me what a virus is."

"Fine," Tander said. "It's nice to know you're not too old to learn something new. My point is . . ." He hesitated and looked at Katha. "No offense, Katha, okay? But let's be reasonable here. This message could be interpreted more than one way."

"Oh, well . . ." Katha started, then for the life of her couldn't think of an intelligent thing to say. "Oh."

"What's with you, Tander?" Vince asked, none too quietly.

"That's what I'm wondering about you, Vince," he

said, his own voice rising. "You're a damned good cop, because you're methodical and careful. You gather your facts and piece them together like an intricate puzzle. When something's missing, you go out and find it. But this?" He waved the paper in the air. "You're plowing in full-steam-ahead. Would you slow down for a minute?"

"There isn't time!"

"The hell there isn't. You're assuming this message is referring to the city welfare system. What if you're wrong? It could be . . . Hell, I don't know. A code name for a computer game some kids are playing, using modems to transmit their current move, or whatever."

Vince muttered an earthy expletive. Tension crackled in the air like electric wires as Vince and Tander glared at each other.

Sirs, Katha thought wildly, pistols will be drawn at ten paces. Please keep the blood off the carpeting.

"Does Katha look like an idiot to you?" Vince yelled. "She deciphered that message for me, and I'm going with exactly what she said. If you don't want in on this one, Ellis, just say so now, and Katha and I will shove off."

Tander opened his mouth, then suddenly closed it again. He looked at Katha, at Vince, back to Katha, then met Vince's dark gaze. A hint of a smile tugged at the corners of his mouth, and a glint of amusement danced in his eyes.

"Okay, Santini," he said, his smile growing bigger, "you win. We'll do this your way. I'm in. In fact, I wouldn't miss this for the world. I'd say"—he chuckled—"that this could be very, very interesting."

What did *that* mean? Katha wondered.

"What does *that* mean?" Vince asked, nearly growling.

"Nothing. Nothing at all," Tander said, all innocence. He handed Katha the paper, then resumed his slouched position in his chair. "Proceed."

Vince stared at Tander for a long moment, as though he were trying to peer inside Tander's brain. The tension in the room had ebbed, tempers cooled. But what if Tander was right? Katha thought. What if she was making a big deal over nothing? How awful. How mortifying.

"Okay," Vince said. "Question. What are the chances of another message coming over Katha's modem?"

"Hard to tell," Tander said, shrugging. "A power surge could have bumped it into Katha's circuit, and it wouldn't happen again. If you're lucky, it's one of those flukes that will recur for no plausible reason. Of course, they'd have to be dumb enough to send something like this over a modem again. The odds aren't terrific, but it's worth covering."

"How?" Vince asked.

"A trace. I've got a nifty little device that will trace every transmission that comes over Katha's modem back to the source, where the call originated from."

"Is that legal?" Katha asked.

Tander looked at her in surprise. "Of course not, sweetheart."

"Oh." She smiled weakly.

"We'll start with that," Vince said. "Katha, what about your father? Don't you want to fill him in on what's going on?"

"Well, I . . . I'll give it some thought," she said, fiddling with the waistband of her sweater.

Vince exchanged a quick look with Tander, then said, "Can you get into the program at the welfare department that has the recipients' addresses and look for the virus?"

"Piece of cake. And I'll give you the device to connect to her modem, but watch your back. These jokers obviously know their computers, and we're operating on the assumption that this scam is for real. There's a slim chance that they've figured out where the misplaced message went. You said that Katha is working out of her father's house. I'd suggest that you pay a discreet visit at night, to put the trace on the modem."

"Good idea," Vince said. "Katha shouldn't be connected with me until we get a better feel for this thing." He draped his arm around her shoulders. "I will take this to the police, but not yet."

Was he, Katha wondered, hesitating to take it to the police because, like Tander, he was wondering if she hadn't completely misinterpreted the message? And why had he put his arm—that strong, warm, comforting arm—around her shoulders? He was driving her crazy. And making her angry. She'd had quite enough of this macho game he was playing with Tander.

"I'd appreciate it, gentlemen," she said stiffly, "if you'd refrain from talking about me as though I weren't in the room. I have a voice, and I intend to be heard. No one comes into my home in the middle of the night without my permission. You'll treat me as an equal partner in this or"—she lifted her chin—"I'll take my crime elsewhere."

Vince opened his mouth, then shook his head and snapped his mouth closed.

Tander roared with laughter. "Santini old buddy, you've met your match. You, chum, have got your hands full."

Three

Vince crept soundlessly into the alley. The night was inky black, a cloud cover blocking the moon and any silvery stars that might have provided some light.

His eyes quickly adjusted to the darkness, and he went on, noting that the houses he passed were silent and dark. No dogs barked to warn of his presence.

The address Katha had given him was in an older, well-kept neighborhood of single story homes. Theirs was the fourth from the corner, she'd said, and he counted as he went.

He was, he thought dryly, skulking in the shadows, despite his claim to Katha that no skulking would take place. She would be waiting for him, as they'd planned, to let him in the back door of the house.

Katha was waiting for him to come home.

For Pete's sake, he chided himself, what a ridiculous thought. His mind was twisting the facts around, giving them false connotations. Then why did it sound so . . . well, so nice? Why was he grinning like an idiot as he skulked around in an alley filled with trash cans? Why wouldn't Katha Logan get out of his mind for longer than ten minutes at a stretch?

Her image had even followed him into the shower that evening. Envisioning her there with him, he had felt hot desire flood through him. It had been easy to imagine pulling her naked body into his arms, kissing her, gently, then ever more passionately, until . . .

Vince shook his head in disgust, then stiffened at a sudden noise. A cat bounded across the alley in front of him and disappeared into the night with an indignant yowl. He started off again, heading for the wooden gate that opened onto Katha's backyard. Stopping outside it, he stared across the yard at the dark house. He was going to go in there, put the trace on the modem, and leave. Strictly business, he told himself firmly. Whatever this strange spell was that Katha had cast on him, he'd had enough. He lived his life alone.

But Katha was waiting for him to come home.

"Santini," he muttered, "shut up."

• • •

Katha sat at the table in the dark kitchen. She was so terribly tense, her muscles were beginning to ache.

Skulking in the shadows, she decided, did not trip her trigger. Skulking was extremely hard on the nerves and could cause a person to feel like a thief-in-the-night in her own home. No more skulking for Katha Logan; she'd leave that to Vince.

Katha sighed. She had sighed a great deal ever since Vince had dropped her off at the restaurant after leaving Tander's yacht. Each time his image danced before her eyes—which was annoyingly often—she sighed. That in itself was ridiculous, as were the jumbled and confusing thoughts tumbling over one another in her poor, befuddled mind.

She sighed again, told herself to knock it off, and shifted in the chair in an attempt to find a more comfortable position.

She had been engaged in a mental battle with herself as they'd left Tander's. A part of her had been awash with warmth, a tingling desire swirling through her at Vince's proximity.

The other section of her being had been jumping up and down, telling her that Vince's possessive attitude had been just an act.

But she'd wanted it to be real!

No. No, she didn't. Absolutely, positively not.

There was no space in her life for a man, for a serious relationship. Even if there were, Vince wasn't a viable candidate. So, she was wasting her time thinking about him and sighing. Therefore, she'd quit. That was simple enough.

She sighed.

"Oh, for crying out loud," she said, shaking her head.

A soft knock sounded at the back door, and she jumped to her feet, nearly knocking over her chair.

"Good heavens," she said, pressing one hand over her racing heart. Darn that Vincent, he'd scared her half to death. So what if she knew he was due any second, he'd still scared her.

She crossed the room and flung open the door. Vince strode in, closed the door with a quiet click, then planted his hands on his hips.

"You didn't even ask who it was," he said.

"Shh. Who else would it be?" she asked, planting *her* hands on *her* hips. "I'm not in the habit of receiving guests who come skulking across my backyard in the dead of night."

"It could have been anyone. You should have checked before you opened the door."

"Shh. It's my door, Mr. Santini, and I'll open it as I see fit."

"Dammit, Katha, you're really ticking me off. This isn't a game we're playing here."

"Oh? Just where does the game end and reality start? Answer me that."

"What are you talking about?"

She started to retort, then caught herself. What a

stupid thing to say, she thought. She wasn't about to tell him how disturbing the game playing on Tander's yacht had been. When was she going to learn to keep her mouth shut?

"Well?" Vince asked.

She dropped her hands to her sides and took a step backward. Vince suddenly seemed too big, too strong, and massive, as he towered over her dressed all in black. He was huge, and beautiful, and he smelled good, and . . .

"Nothing," she said quietly. "Just forget I said that. I'll show you where my office is so you can put the device on the modem."

Vince frowned down at her. She seemed so small, he mused, so fragile and vulnerable. She'd taken him on toe-to-toe, yet now was backing away, withdrawing into herself. He shouldn't have yelled at her, jumped all over her without even saying hello. She wasn't a trained police officer, trained for clandestine rendezvous. She was probably incredibly nervous, maybe even scared. Damn, he was such a louse sometimes.

"Hey," he said gently. He lifted his hands and framed her face, his thumbs stroking her soft cheeks. "Look, I . . . Katha. Oh, hell."

With that, he lowered his head and kissed her.

Katha stiffened in shock and flattened her hands on Vince's hard chest. She was determined to push him away and tell him that he was arrogant for presuming he could kiss her simply because *he'd* decided he wanted to. But as his tongue slipped between her lips to meet hers, the thought fled into oblivion.

Her hands slid upward, savoring the feel of his strong muscles, her fingertips inching into his thick black hair. He encircled her body with his arms and drew her against him.

This, he thought hazily, was what he'd been waiting for. This kiss, the feel of Katha's slender body nestled against his, had been an eternity in coming, but Lord, it had been worth the wait. She tasted like sweet nectar, and as she swayed against him, pressing herself closer, the blood pounded in his veins. His passion flared into a raging fire.

He'd anticipated the ecstasy of the kiss, and now he wanted more. He wanted all of her. His mind was racing forward with visions of her naked beneath him, her auburn curls a vivid halo around her face, her eyes smoky with desire for him, only him.

He wrapped his arms even tighter around her, his tongue delving farther into her mouth in a steady rhythm. A groan rumbled in his chest.

Desire like nothing she'd ever known whirled within Katha. Her breasts were heavy, crushed to Vince's chest in a sweet pain that she knew could only be soothed by his strong but gentle hands. Her legs trembled, and a pulsing deep within her matched the rhythm of his tongue stroking hers.

She was acutely aware of every inch of her being, and even her skin tingled with sensations. Everything was magnified. The taste of Vince, the magnificent power of him, the aroma of his soap, his after-shave, and the heady scent that was thoroughly male. His body was rugged where hers was softly curved; two pieces of a puzzle fitting perfectly together. And pressing against her was the hard evidence of his desire for her.

Or *was* it a desire for her, Katha Logan? The scene on Tander's yacht replayed in her mind, and she remembered that she'd vowed not to fall prey to his little game.

She dropped her hands back to his chest and pushed. The forceful action caused him to release her, and she backed away until she thudded against the counter. She drew in an unsteady breath, but made no attempt to speak as she willed the heated trembling in her body to quiet.

Vince blinked and shook his head, then returned to reality with a thud that cooled his ardor, leaving him confused and frustrated. He stared at Katha, able to see her in the darkness as clearly as if the room were ablaze with light. She slowly met his gaze, a stricken expression on her face. Her lips were slightly parted, seeming to invite him to smother them with his. He curled his hands into fists to keep from reaching out and pulling her into his embrace once again.

"What . . ." His voice was rough with passion, and he cleared his throat. "What's wrong?"

"That shouldn't have happened," she whispered.

"Why the hell not?" he asked loudly. "It was inevitable, Katha, and you know it. There's been something brewing between us from the beginning. It's been building, threatening to explode. You wanted that kiss as much as I did."

"No—"

"And you wanted *me*. I felt it, felt you giving more of yourself. And Lord knows," he went on, raking a hand through his hair, "you were able to tell how much *I* wanted *you*." He paused. "Dammit, quit looking at me like you're scared to death of me. I didn't take anything from you that you weren't offering. That kiss was equally shared. We came within an ace of making love too."

"We certainly did not! That kiss should never have happened, and it won't be repeated."

He stepped forward and braced his hands on the counter on either side of her, trapping her. His body was inches from hers, and when he spoke his voice was low and controlled.

"Won't it?" he asked, looking directly into her eyes. "Are you so very certain of that? If I kissed you right now, wouldn't you respond to me again, just as you did before?"

"No. I . . . No." He had to move away from her! She could feel the heat emanating from his body, and the desire still pulsing within her responded to it. He had to move. "Go away."

"Not a chance," he said, and covered her mouth with his.

The kiss was rough, seeming to steal the very breath from her body and every thought from her mind. She could only feel. Savor. And *want* Vince Santini. Her tongue met his, her body met his, her passion rose once again to heights never known to her before. She moaned softly, giving more, taking more, and wanting more.

The kiss gentled as Vince drank in her sweet taste, filling his senses with her essence, feeling his arousal grow hard and heavy as the kiss went on and on.

But then, in the far recesses of his passion-laden mind, a niggling echo gained volume. It was Katha's earlier words, when she'd demanded to know where the game ended and reality began. What game? What in the hell was she talking about? There were no games being played here.

He lifted his head and smacked the switch on the wall, bringing the room alive with bright light. He blinked several times, then frowned as he looked at Katha. She slowly opened her eyes, then squinted against the glare.

"Why did you turn on the light?" she asked breathlessly.

"Pretend you got up for a glass of milk," he said gruffly. "There's nothing unusual about someone going into the kitchen in the middle of the night." Lord, she was beautiful. Her lips were moist and appeared thoroughly kissed . . . by him, which was the way it should be. Her hair was in appealing disarray from his fingers weaving through it. The flush on her cheeks, the smokiness in her eyes, spoke of her desire for him. And only him.

"I want an answer from you about what you said earlier."

"What did I say?" she asked, gazing at him dreamily.

"Katha, come on, snap out of it. This is very important."

"You bet," she said, bobbing her head up and down.

"Wonderful," he muttered. "Katha, please, listen to me. What did you mean before when you asked where the game playing ended and reality started?"

"Oh, that." She waved one hand breezily in the air. "I was just blithering. Don't give it another thought." Because she had no intention of explaining, she added silently. No such words would pass her lips. She turned off the kitchen light. "A person only needs so much time to drink a glass of milk. Terrific, now I can't see a thing. We'll have to wait until my eyes readjust to the darkness before I can take you to my office. I'll clobber myself on the furniture if I try to walk through the house now."

"My eyes adapt quickly to darkness, so if you tell me where your office . . . No, now hold it." He paused and stroked one thumb over her lips. "You *did* say that, Katha," he went on, a warmer tone to his voice, "about playing games. I really don't know what you meant, but I *do* know there are no games being played between us about anything. Talk to me. Don't pretend you never said those words."

Katha sighed, despite her vow to stop doing that. "Vince, I'm tired. It's been a very long day, and now we're using up the night. I need some sleep. Couldn't we just put the gizmo on the modem and be done with it for now? I'm really exhausted."

Damn, he thought, she wasn't going to tell him what she'd meant. Not now, anyway. But as far as he was concerned, the subject wasn't settled, nor forgotten. It could go on the back burner for the night, but he had every intention of getting to the bottom of it. Soon.

"All right, Katha, we'll get this done, then I'll be on my way so you can get some sleep. In just a few minutes I'll be out of here."

He didn't have to sound so cheerful about it, Katha thought. Having him there certainly wasn't a grim experience by any means. Those kisses had been . . . Oh, Lord, they'd been unbelievable. A tad frightening when she realized how much she responded to him, but exciting and . . . She'd better tell her mind to change the subject.

"I can see well enough now," she said. "Follow me."

"Your father must be a very sound sleeper. Are you sure we're not disturbing him? Or did you explain to him that I'd be here?"

"No, I didn't tell him anything. He won't wake up." She started across the kitchen. "Coming?"

"Yes." And that was another thing, he thought. There was something odd about Katha's reluctance to speak about her father. If they were partners in

Logan and Logan Typing Service, didn't the man have the right to know what was going on? There was a secret section to Katha, and the entrance to it was tightly guarded. All in due time, Santini, he told himself. Take it slow and easy. "I'm right behind you, Katha. You can't get rid of me easily, you know. I'm sticking to you like glue."

What a delicious thought, she mused. They'd be just like two peas in a pod. Oh, knock it off, Katha.

Her office was at the end of a hall, and Vince surmised the large room had originally been a bedroom. He took a small pen flashlight from his jacket pocket, and following the instructions Tander had given him, inserted a silver disk the size of a quarter into one end of the modem receiver.

"There," he said.

"That's all there is to it? Tander could have given it to me to put in there."

Vince shook his head. "It's my responsibility. Now, starting tomorrow save all the printouts that come over your modem."

"I will. Vince, did you give any further thought to what Tander said about the message I received just being kids playing a game, or something equally harmless?"

"No. He stated his case. I rejected it. That's the end of it." Vince ignored the little voice in his head reminding him that he hadn't believed Katha at first either.

"But what if—"

"No." He turned and left the office, and Katha followed.

At the kitchen door, he stopped and pushed his hands into his jacket pockets. "Well, now you can get some sleep. Oh, here." He took a card from his pocket and gave it to her. "My home phone number is on there, and Tander's number on the yacht if you can't reach me."

"Okay."

"Katha, I . . ." He stiffened. "Shh. I think I hear something."

"I don't hear—"

"Stay put. I'll have a look around outside."

"But—" Before she could speak further, Vince had slipped out the back door. She strained her ears for any sound coming from the yard, but heard nothing more than the echo of her own pounding heart.

Suddenly Vince's voice boomed in the distance.

"Hey!" he yelled. "Hold it right there. I have a gun. Don't be stupid."

Oh, Lord, Katha thought frantically. Please be careful, Vince. He had a gun. Did the other person have one? Vince . . .

There was a loud crash, then the roar of a motorcycle, fading quickly up the alley.

That's enough, Katha thought. She wasn't staying in that house for another second, wondering what was happening to Vince.

She opened the door and ran outside, just as Vince came back through the gate. They met in the middle of the grassy yard. Vince pulled a handkerchief from his pocket and pressed it to the side of his forehead.

"Who was that?" she asked. "What happened? Are you bleeding? Why are you bleeding? Do you want me to call the paramedics? Take you to the hospital?"

"Whoa. I just have a small cut, that's all. He flung a trash can at me, and the lid flew off and clipped me. I don't know who he was, or if he has anything to do with what we're involved in. It could have been a kid out joyriding, and he'd just stopped to adjust something on his bike. Hell, I don't know."

"Come inside so I can look at your head. The whole world knows we're skulking around now. There's no reason why I can't turn on lights and tend to that cut."

"I suppose you're right." Vince stared into the darkness in the direction the motorcycle had gone. "Coincidences make me edgy. I don't like this, Katha, not one damn bit."

Four

Vince walked across the empty office, nodding as he glanced around. At the door, he peered into the small outer area, then walked back to the wall of sparkling windows that afforded a far-reaching view of the city.

A heavy smog hung in the air, and from eight floors up, he could only assume the busy streets below were really there. He turned around again and shoved his hands into the back pockets of his jeans as he surveyed the large carpeted room.

This, he thought, a smile beginning to form on his lips, was the office of Vincent Santini, Private Investigator, and it was a helluva classy place. Or, it would be once he got some furniture in there.

A frown replaced the smile. He didn't know the

first thing about decorating. He'd bought his apartment with the furniture included, moved in and that was that. He hadn't ever considered if the decor was to his liking.

But this office had to be just right. It had to evoke confidence in would-be clients without being so austere that it turned them off. They had to be comfortable, relaxed, so they'd open up and tell him what was on their mind.

"Hello?" a voice called from the outer office.

"Yes," Vince answered.

"Telephone company," a man said, appearing in the doorway. "I have a work order here to check the phone jacks. Are you"—he glanced at a paper in his hand—"Vincent Santini?"

"Yep."

"Okay, we're in business. I'll get to it."

Maybe *that* guy was in business, Vince thought wryly, but Vincent Santini, Private Investigator, was missing a few necessary ingredients to qualify as being in business. Little things like furniture, someone to answer the phone, his name on the door, and clients.

No, that wasn't entirely true. He had a client. Katha Logan.

He smiled as he ran his fingertip over the small cut on the side of his forehead. She'd fussed and fluttered all over him when they'd gone back into the house the night before. She'd brought out enough first-aid equipment to patch up a wounded platoon, waved him onto a kitchen chair, and went about her nursing chore with an adorable seriousness.

He'd loved every minute of it.

It had been a long time since anyone had focused on him like that, treated him as though he were the most important thing in their life. He'd had to curl his hands into tight fists to keep from pulling her onto his lap and covering her soft, sweet lips once again with his.

The kisses they'd shared had been sensational. Lord, how he'd wanted her. Instantly. Just thinking about those kisses, the feel of her slender body nestled to his, caused desire to tighten within him.

Easy, Santini, he told himself. He could live without having the telephone guy being witness to his body's arousal as he remembered holding, kissing, caressing Katha Logan.

She was his client, he thought, firmly pulling his thoughts back under his control. A nonpaying client, yes, but still a client and nothing more. Granted, he wasn't behaving entirely properly around her, staying on the impersonal straight and narrow, but that was understandable. Katha's case was his first as a private investigator. It stood to reason that he had to adjust to his new role. He'd get a handle on it. No problem.

"Vince?"

His head snapped up, and his heart started a

drumroll cadence. Katha. Standing in the doorway in a beige sweater and a flared tweed skirt, she was beautiful. Her hair was a soft halo around her face, her lips . . . Oh, Katha.

"I'm sorry," she said, smiling. "Did I startle you? You look a little shell-shocked." And gorgeous, she thought, always gorgeous. In jeans and a pearly gray V-neck sweater over a pale gray dress shirt, he was simply gorgeous. If Vince knew about the sensuous, wanton dreams she'd had of him after he'd left her the previous night, she would dissolve into a puddle of embarrassment. "May I come in? You did say that I was to meet you at your new office."

"What?" He shook his head. "Oh, sure, come on in."

She walked in slowly, glancing around. "This is going to be marvelous, Vince. It's so big, and the windows will make it sunny and bright . . . except when it's smoggy like today."

"Excuse me," the telephone man said. "You're all set, Mr. Santini. You have the jacks you need. Just bring your phones in and plug them in. Sign here and I'll call in the order to turn the juice on."

Vince scribbled his name on the offered paper, thanked the man, then watched him leave the office. A silence fell over the room, and he slowly shifted his gaze to meet Katha's.

Oh, good grief, Katha thought, feeling a heated, curling sensation low inside her. Vince's dark eyes were radiating a blatant message of desire, of pure, hungry want. What did he see in *her* eyes? This was insane. A few kisses shared in the dead of night shouldn't have such a potent, lingering effect in the light of a new day. But then, what did *she* know? She'd only had one lover and was inexperienced to the point of ridiculous.

She shouldn't have kissed him, but, oh, those kisses had been wondrous. She shouldn't have responded with such abandon, but she had felt so alive when he'd held her in his arms. She shouldn't be standing there wishing that he would swoop her right back into his arms again and kiss the living daylights out of her.

She shouldn't even allow such thoughts to skitter through her mind. Yet why did he have to be so far away when he had *that* look in those mesmerizing eyes of his?

"Katha," he said hoarsely. "I . . ."

"Yes?" She hoped her voice hadn't really sounded that breathless and quivering.

"I . . . What do you think of fish tanks?" He stared at a spot on the wall behind her, somewhere just above her head.

Fish tanks? Tanks of fish? Was that some sort of bizarre sexual question? Would she find herself in a heap of trouble if she gave him the wrong answer?

"Fish tanks?" she repeated.

"Yeah. I have these friends, Joy and Declan Harris. Joy is a psychologist, and she has a sharp looking fish tank built into the wall of her office. I was thinking . . . No, I guess not. I don't know the first thing about taking care of fish. Forget it." He glanced around. "I have to decorate this place."

A giggle escaped from Katha. "We're talking about decorating? Well, fancy that. Fish tanks are nice. The talents of fish are a tad limited, I suppose, but if you're into watching great swimming then . . ." She shrugged. "Is that why you asked me to meet you here? To discuss fish tanks?"

"No. I wanted to talk to you, and since no one knows about this office yet, I felt it was a safe enough place. I've been giving a great deal of thought to our situation. I don't think either of us enjoy meetings in the middle of the night. Also, I'm concerned that there's even a chance that these would-be thieves have discovered where their wayward transmission went and might be watching you. So I thought if you and I were seeing each other socially . . . you know, going out, dating, it would make perfect sense for me to come to your house. That way I can keep a better eye on what's going on. And after the incident in the alley last night, I really believe this is a better plan."

"Vince, the boy on the motorcycle was fourteen years old."

"What?"

"His father brought him to the house this morning. The kid was so shook up because you yelled that you had a gun, he confessed all when he got home last night. He lives one block over from me. The motorcycle belongs to his eighteen-year-old brother, and the younger boy took it for a ride without permission. His father made him apologize for any inconvenience he'd caused, and he also promised never to do it again. So, you see, it was nothing to be concerned about."

Vince frowned. "Oh. Well, that's good news." It was? Of course it was. "But I still feel my new plan is best." Absolutely. *He* was running this show. "I'll be very visible. We'll put this into operation this evening by going out to dinner. Wear something dressy, and I'll go so far as to put on a suit and tie. If someone's keeping an eye on you, I'll appear to be simply the latest man in your life."

What an exciting, delicious scenario that was, Katha mused. Vince was her man, her significant other, her lover—Katha, stop it. This was business, strictly business. But such sacrifices she was making in the name of justice.

"Why the smile?" Vince asked.

"What? Oh, nothing. I was just thinking about what you said. We're going to act out parts, right? Sort of like when I grabbed you in front of city hall and got you away from those reporters, pretending to be your . . . whatever."

"Well, yes, I guess you could say we're like actors in a play." This was his idea, and now he didn't like the sound of it. She was going to put on a pretty dress and smile and laugh with him, but it really wasn't going to be for him. Lord, what a stupid plan. Well, he was stuck with it now, less than a genius that he was. "I'll pick you up at eight o'clock," he tacked on gruffly.

"That's fine," Katha said. More game playing, she thought, and now she'd agreed to be a part of it. Vince would have no difficulty in his role of the attentive lover. She'd seen him in action on Tander's yacht. The scenario was rapidly losing its appeal. In fact, she hated it. "I'll be ready." She busied herself picking an imaginary bit of lint off her sweater.

"All right. Katha, listen, there's something else we should cover. It's about last night and the kisses—"

"No," she said sharply, her gaze meeting his again. "I don't want to discuss what happened. It's done, over."

"Is it?"

"Yes, of course. It was the middle of the night, the situation was unusual, even weird, if you ask me. I . . . We were victims of circumstances not remotely close to normal." She smiled brightly. "Yes, exactly. That's the explanation for what happened. There's no need to dwell on it further. We'll just chalk it up as one of those strange things best forgotten. Right?"

He started slowly toward her. "Bull."

"Oh," she said, her smile fading. "I was afraid of

that." She watched him come closer . . . and closer, then held up one hand. "Halt!"

"You can't say that," he said, still advancing. "*I'm* the cop, remember?"

"Okay, then try this on for size. Do not enter my space, Santini. That's yuppie jargon for 'If you come near me, I'm going to punch you in the nose.' "

He laughed and kept right on coming.

"Oh, help," Katha mumbled.

He stopped in front of her, all traces of laughter gone. He slid one hand to the nape of her neck, his thumb lightly tracing the line of her jaw, then up over the smooth skin of her cheek. She shivered.

"Oh, Vince, don't," she said, gazing into his eyes. "I'm just not cut out for these kinds of games. Can't you see that? Don't you realize that I'm not like the women you know? Going to dinner with you and pretending to be romantically involved is one thing, but when we're alone like this, I just can't deal with the games. Yes, I was engaged, but that was a long time ago, and there hasn't been . . . What I mean is, I don't . . ."

"Sleep around?" He continued the sensual caressing with his thumb. "It never occurred to me that you did. And if you're saying you've only had one lover, the guy you were engaged to, that doesn't surprise me in the least. As for playing games? You keep bringing that up, but you won't explain what you mean. I get the feeling you think *I* play games, and I don't."

"Maybe it's a subjective term. Your definition of game playing is probably poles apart from mine. Vince, we operate on different planes, that's all. Men like you and Tander march to a drummer who's beating a tune I've never even heard."

"Tander? What does he have to do with this? I thought we were talking about us?" His jaw tightened. "You'd prefer to discuss Tander, is that it?"

"No! I don't want to talk about this at all." She paused. "Was there more we needed to discuss about our investigation while I'm here?" There, she thought. She'd switched to a nice, safe topic. She'd revealed more of herself than she'd intended to, but at least now she was back on firm ground. How humiliating to have told Vince she'd only had one lover. She certainly turned into Miss Chatter-Cheeks when she was around Vince Santini. "Well? Was there anything else that you wanted?"

"Wrong question," he said, then lowered his head and captured her mouth with his.

Finally, Katha thought dreamily. It had taken him forever to get to this. Oh, heavens, what was she doing? She wasn't supposed to kiss this man. But then again . . . Oh, never mind. This was Vince, and the kiss was wonderful, and she'd worry about everything else later. Much later.

She lifted her arms to encircle his neck. He drew her close to his body, his hands spread across her back. Her breasts were crushed against his chest as his tongue delved into her mouth, stroking hers, dancing and dueling with it. Their passions soared.

Dammit, Vince thought, what was he doing? He'd told himself he'd correct his behavior with Katha. He was a detective, and Katha was his client. Why was he kissing her? Because he couldn't have stopped himself even if someone had had a gun pointed at his head. He needed to kiss her, hold her in his arms and savor her soft, gently curved body.

He raised his head to draw a quick breath, then took her lips again, feeling her respond to him, give of herself, surrender to him . . .

He stiffened and dropped his arms to his sides. Turning, he strode to the windows and stared at the yellowish smog. Though his heart still beat wildly, he willed his aroused body back under his control. Confusing thoughts and emotions slammed against one another, leaving him confused and causing his head to throb.

Katha stared at the rigid set to Vince's back and shoulders as she drew a steadying breath. What was wrong with him? she wondered. One moment he was kissing her like there was no tomorrow, and the next he was way over there, anger emanating from him. What a complicated man. Well, he could just explain his actions to her. She had enough trouble understanding why she behaved the way *she* did around him, let alone understanding *him*. He was going to overload her circuits.

"Vince," she said, amazed her voice sounded normal, "it's obvious that you're angry about something and I don't have the foggiest idea what. I *do* know that I'm terribly confused."

He spun around, his dark eyes flashing, a pulse beating rapidly in his temple. She took a step backward without realizing she'd done it.

"*You're* confused?" His sharp bark of laughter held no trace of amusement. "Let me tell you something, lady, you don't know what confusion is." He pointed one long finger at her. "You're doing tricky things to my mind, weaving some kind of spell around me, making me totally lose it when I'm around you and, dammit, I want it stopped."

A single thought came to the surface of Katha's befuddled mind, bringing with it a one-word response to his tirade.

"Huh?"

Vince mumbled a coarse expletive and stared up at the ceiling for a long moment, attempting to rein in his frustration. Katha stared at him and forced herself not to back up even farther when he met her gaze again.

"Don't give me 'Huh'," he said tightly. "You know exactly what I'm talking about. You keep insinuating that some kind of game playing is going on here. I'm beginning to think that *you're* the one playing games, Ms. Logan." Hell, Santini, what a stupid thing to say. Katha didn't know the first thing about game playing between men and women. He was angry at himself and taking it out on her. He was such a sleazeball. "No, wait a minute. I—"

"No, you wait a minute, mister," she said, volume on high. "I've had quite enough of your quicksilver mood switches and nasty accusations."

"I—"

"Cut," she said, slicing one hand through the air. "I'm speaking and, buster, you'd better listen."

Uh-oh, Vince thought. Now he'd done it. She was mad as hell. And beautiful, so damn beautiful. Her eyes were like laser beams, her cheeks were flushed, and her lips were still moist and swollen from the kisses they'd shared.

"Santini," she went on, snapping him back to attention, "I'm not playing games because I don't know how to play the games you're playing. I was there, remember? On Tander's yacht? I was the pawn you two did your little vaudeville routine on. 'She's mine, Tander.' 'You bet, Vince. No problem.' You hovered around me with your phony possessiveness like a kid on the playground protecting his basketball. Games, Vince? You're a pro, and so is Tander, but leave me out of it. And leave me alone."

"That's what you've meant? You think that the way I acted on Tander's yacht was a game?"

"Of course it was. I knew it then, and I know it now. I'm furious with myself for kissing you the way I do every time you get a notion in your head to kiss me. I can't seem to help it. I just do it, and it's so wonderful, and I feel so—No! No more. You're a private investigator, and I'm your client, even if I'm not paying you. It's not going to matter one iota that I think about you when we're apart, and have dreams about you that you wouldn't believe, and . . ." She sighed and threw up her hands. "And I wonder if when I grow up I'll learn to keep my mouth shut, or if I'll be a blithering idiot until I'm old and gray."

"Katha . . ."

"Oh, be quiet," she said, then sniffled. She folded her arms tightly beneath her breasts, lifted her chin, and sniffled again.

"Please," he said quietly, "listen to me, Katha. I didn't mean what I said about you playing games. I know you wouldn't do that. I was angry at myself because I'd just given myself another lecture on my lack of professional conduct around you, and then proceeded to ignore everything I'd told myself."

Katha pressed her lips together and blinked several times against threatening tears.

"I don't know what it is about you," he went on. "I think about you, too, when we're not together, and when we are, my good intentions take a flying leap. When I'm near you, I'm consumed with the need to hold and kiss you. I want you, Katha Logan. I want to make slow, sweet love to you for hours. I don't understand what's happening here, but it could possibly, if not nipped in the bud, lead to something serious. I wasn't playing games on Tander's yacht. Everything I did and said was honest, and it surprised the hell out of me."

He ran one hand over the back of his neck.

"Katha, I told you that I don't want any part of a committed relationship, and I meant it. I want to make love with you, but I have no intention of *falling* in love with you. That just isn't in the cards for me, not now or ever. I'm being as truthful with you as I can find the words to be. I'm alone, and plan to remain alone. I don't know why I constantly lose control around you, but I intend to get a handle on it. And I swear to you that nothing I've done, or said, has been phony, or part of some macho game."

Katha nodded, not trusting herself to speak for fear that the tears pressing against the back of her eyes would spill over. Why she felt so depressed, she didn't know. She wasn't in a position to have a serious relationship herself, and she was certain Vince was being truthful when he said he hadn't been playing games with her. At least her battered ego had been soothed. She hadn't been a pawn on Tander's yacht after all. Vince was saying everything she should be relieved to hear. Then why was she a breath away from bursting into tears?

"Would you," she said, deciding to run the risk of speaking, "prefer that I take the evidence I have about the virus to the police?"

"No. I'm in on this, and I'm staying in. We understand each other better now, I think. We're strongly attracted to each other. There's nothing unusual about that. How far we take it will be a mutually agreed upon decision, and no one gets hurt. Okay?"

"Oh, yes, fine. Sure, Vince, okay. Communication is everything those talk-show people say it is, isn't it? We're all squared away." And she'd never felt so hollow and miserable in her entire life.

"Great," he said. "We're all set." And for two cents, he'd walk out of that room and into the nearest mental hospital, because he'd obviously lost his mind.

Five

"You really should have this place redecorated, Vince," Tander said. "This ultra-modern chrome and glass decor just isn't you, even if it is state-of-the-art stuff. Don't you agree, Declan?"

Declan Harris glanced around the spacious living room. "I do, indeed. Vince leans more toward the rumpled corduroy look or faded jeans."

Vince chuckled as he handed each of the men a cold can of beer.

"See what I mean?" Declan said. "Tacky, Santini, very tacky."

Vince shrugged. "So, don't drink it." He slumped down into a black leather chair, stretched out his legs, and crossed them at the ankle.

"It's not *that* tacky," Declan said. "After the workout we put in at the health club, this will be heaven going down my throat." He paused. "Even if I don't have a chilled, frosted glass to drink it from."

"Stuff it," Vince said pleasantly.

Declan and Tander laughed, then all of them took deep swallows of beer.

The three men were close friends, and each was well-built and handsome. Like Vince, Declan had dark hair, but his eyes were a brilliant green. Tander's light brown, sun-streaked hair was in vivid contrast to the other two.

Vince and Tander had known each other for more than fifteen years. Declan was the newcomer, having met Vince a few years earlier, when Vince was investigating threats made on Declan's life after his partner in his architectural firm died. When Vince introduced Declan and Tander, the two men had hit it off instantly. Whenever Tander docked in L.A., the three got together. The last time he'd been there, six months earlier, he and Vince had been Declan's groomsmen when he married Joy Barlow.

"Joy sends her love to both of you," Declan said lazily as he sprawled on the sofa. "I said she should send her 'like,' because I've cornered the market on her love, but she said she was sending her 'love.' I refused to agree to give either of you a hug and a kiss."

Vince laughed. "Well, damn."

"Don't worry," Tander said, winking at Vince. "We'll get them from her in person next time we see her."

"Maybe a handshake," Declan said with mock ferocity, then grinned. "Anyway," he went on, "Joy wishes you well in your new career, Vince, and suggested we all go out to dinner to celebrate your fresh challenge. Watch your stress level, pal. Major changes in your life can cause massive stress, if you're not careful."

"Oh, Lord," Tander said, "here we go again. We're in for another lecture by Declan Harris on stress management. Why don't you leave that stuff to your beautiful wife? She's the expert."

"Well, I've learned a lot about it from Joy. But I'll give you a break today. I want to hear about this case you're working on, Vince. You said at the health club that you'd fill me in once we got back here. And, yes, I know that nothing said leaves this room. Speak."

"Okay," Vince said. "Here it is in a nutshell." He gave Declan a brief summary of what had taken place since the message had inadvertently come over Katha's modem. "Get it?" he finished.

Declan nodded. "It's a beaut. This Katha Logan really stumbled into a hornet's nest. That's quite an operation, and one helluva lot of money they're fixing to get their hands on. A lot of people will be in trouble if those checks don't arrive when they're supposed to."

"Mmm," Tander said, and drained his beer can.

Vince glared at him. "Don't say it, Tander."

"Say what?" Declan asked, looking between the two men. "What am I missing here?"

"Mr. Ellis," Vince said, shooting Tander another dark look, "seems to feel that Katha's message could be interpreted any number of ways, including kids playing computer games. I totally disagree."

"No joke," Tander said. "You're charging ahead like a bull going after a red flag. And what have you got? Nothing. I've checked out the people working in the welfare department, and they're clean as a whistle. One big-time crook on the payroll had a speeding ticket a couple of years ago, and another got caught with expired tags on his license plates. We're talking about major criminals here, boys. High-flying crime."

"I can do without your sarcasm, Tander," Vince said. "That message is as clear as a bell."

"Mmm," Tander said. "I love the bit about the 'dangerous criminal' in the alley being a kid who copped his brother's motorcycle. That's choice."

"Give it a rest," Vince said. "You have the right to your opinion, but keep it to yourself."

"This is fascinating," Declan said. "You two obviously are seeing this from opposite sides."

Tander shrugged. "It's Vince's case. I'm just along for the ride, helping out where I can, doing what I'm told. What's next up, Santini?"

"I have to give thought to how we can search for the virus in the program without raising suspicion. I don't want those yo-yos to split because they got nervous when someone came sniffing around. In the meantime, I'm staying close to Katha in case the creeps have discovered where their transmission went. I'm taking her out to dinner tonight, very open, very visible. I'm hoping, if they *are* watching her, that they'll think I'm just the latest man in her life, and not place any emphasis on my being a detective if they tag me."

Tander whooped with laughter. "You're going to stay close to Katha for the sake of the investigation? Santini, who do you think you're kidding?"

"Ah," Declan said, "I've got a feeling Katha Logan is a beautiful woman."

"Got it in one," Tander said, grinning. "And our man here has gone a mite deranged over her."

Declan grinned. "The plot thickens."

"I call 'em as I see 'em," Tander said. He got to his feet. "Come on, Declan, let's go. We'll leave Vince to scrub and rub his decrepit body so he'll smell good and be all squeaky clean for Katha. Gonna wear a tie, Vince? It's been so long since you've duded up, do you want me to hang around and fix the knot for you? You've probably forgotten how."

"Good-bye, Ellis," Vince said. "Don't call me, I'll call you."

"Keep me posted, Vince," Declan said, following Tander across the room. "This is great stuff. Oh, and remember to watch for any signs of stress."

Vince shook his head as the pair disappeared out the door.

Damn that Tander, he fumed. He was like a dog who'd found a bone and now wouldn't let go. Stubborn man. The message that had come over Katha's modem was exactly what Katha surmised it to be. He was proceeding on that premise, and he was right, by damn. He didn't have time to mess around with something that was a maybe. He had a new business to get off the ground, an office to decorate, and . . . and Tander was full of bull with his crazy ideas about kids playing a computer game.

"Hell," he muttered. He stood and headed for the bedroom. "Scrub and rub my decrepit body. Ellis, put a cork in it."

Vince's less-than-chipper mood had not improved by the time he parked in front of Katha's house. His frown deepened as he got out of the car.

There was an old vehicle parked just ahead of him. It was nearly void of paint, rusted in spots, and had to be at least thirty years old. He made a mental note of the license number, then went up the front walk.

On the porch he patted the knot of his tie, sent a smug mental message to Tander that Vincent Santini could still create a perfect four-in-hand, and knocked on the door.

Moments later, Katha opened it, soft light from the living room pouring over her.

"Hello, Vince," she said, and stepped back. "Come

in." Oh, yes, she thought, do come right on in. In his resplendent attire of a dark suit, crisp white shirt, and paisley tie, a matching handkerchief in his top pocket, he was just the man she wanted to come through her door to see her. The man was absolutely breathtaking. "You're right on time."

"Hello," Vince said, entering the house. "Do you happen to know who owns the car that's . . ." His gaze slid over Katha as she closed the door and turned to face him. The image of the dilapidated vehicle fled his mind and was replaced by the lovely woman before him.

She was wearing a fitted black suit, the slim skirt falling just to her knees. The jacket had padded shoulders, wide white lapels, and a white belt that accentuated her narrow waist. Her only jewelry were discreet gold earrings and a heart-shaped locket on a gold chain.

She was beautiful, he thought, staring at her. She was sensational. And he knew there was no way he'd be able to keep his hands off her.

"You're . . . " He stopped at the hoarseness in his voice, then tried again. "You're beautiful, Katha. You look . . . I've never . . . That dress is . . . Well, hell."

"Thank you," she said, smiling. "I'll decipher all of that as being a compliment. You look very . . . nice, too, Vince. I've never seen you in anything but jeans before. You're marvelous in a suit. And I like your tie. You certainly do a perfect four-in-hand. Some men mess up the knot in their tie and spoil the whole effect." Do *not* blither on, Katha Logan, she told herself. And do not leap into the man's arms, or drool on his shirtfront. "Anyway, you're very hand-some."

He wanted to kiss her, Vince thought foggily. He *needed* to kiss her. By damn, he was *going* to kiss her. Right now.

He took a step toward her.

"What were you saying about a car?" she asked, halting his advance.

"Car?" he repeated. "What car?"

He stared blankly at her for a moment. "The car. Oh, yes, the car." He cleared his throat. "There's an old heap parked at the curb. I just wondered if you knew who it belonged to." Not that he gave a damn at the moment. He wanted to kiss her!

"Old heap!" a voice behind him said. He whirled in surprise. "Young man, that is a vintage automo-bile, I'll have you know. Don't you recognize a classic Studebaker when you see one?"

Vince opened his mouth to reply, realized he had no idea what to say, then scrutinized the diminutive woman who was crossing the room.

She was all of five feet tall, had a curly cap of snow-white hair, and appeared to be close to sev-enty. She was wearing a lacy dress that he was certain was yellowed by age, not by design, and which could have doubled as a tablecloth. Perched on her head was a bizarre, square hat; bright red, with a tall purple tulip that bobbed this way and that as she walked. It was as though she'd stepped out of another era, he thought. All she needed was a name like Mabel, or Ethel, or Gertrude.

"Now, Martha . . ." Katha started.

Ah-ha. Martha. Close enough. Score one for the Italian kid from L.A.

". . . Vince didn't mean to be disrespectful of your car," Katha went on. "Did you, Vince? No, of course not. Martha Turnbull, I'd like you to meet Vincent Santini. Vince, I'd like you to meet Martha Turnbull, an old and dear friend of my father."

"Ma'am," Vince said, dipping his head, "it's my pleasure. Please forgive me for any derogatory remark made toward your . . . classic vehicle. It's dark outside, and I didn't get a clear view of it."

"Well," Martha said, with a sniff. "I'll forgive you because you're obviously Katha's beau." She smiled. "I do declare, Katha, you may be a late bloomer, but you've made up splendidly for lost time." She did a slow and thorough perusal of Vince from head to toe, then nodded in approval. "Nice bod."

Vince chuckled as Katha's cheeks flushed pink with embarrassment.

"Oh, good heavens," she said, rolling her eyes.

"Thank you, ma'am," Vince said solemnly to Martha. "It's very comforting to know that my bod passes your inspection."

"It certainly does," Martha said, beaming. She patted her curls, then gave the top of her hat a solid whack. The tulip bounced precariously back and forth. "Well, I'm off. Katha, Bobby looks so good tonight. Jane said he's eating better and sleeping like an old log. I wore this hat because it has always been Bobby's favorite, and he was so pleased. Well, ta-ta, children. Have a wonderful evening."

Martha kissed Katha on the cheek, smiled at Vince and gave him yet another scrutiny, then bustled out the door.

A silence fell over the room. Katha busied herself fluffing and straightening two throw pillows on the sofa. Vince watched her for a minute, frowning once more.

"Katha?" he said finally.

She sighed, then turned to face him. "You have questions," she said quietly. "Bobby . . . Robert Logan is my father, the other half of Logan and Logan Typing Service. I—I moved home and added his name to my company when he . . . had a stroke. He's completely bedridden because he's paralyzed on one side."

"Damn, Katha, I'm sorry. Why didn't you tell me sooner?"

She lifted her chin and met his gaze directly. "I love my father, Vince. He was my idol, my hero, while I was growing up. He's a proud man who worked hard all of his life. He always told me that a man's pride, his sense of self-worth, was a precious thing, and he should live his life so that he never tarnished that pride in himself."

Vince nodded. "Go on."

"When I moved back in here, the man I was engaged to found my father, his condition, repulsive. He couldn't stand to be in the same room with Dad. He said I'd have to put my father in a nursing home before we were married. I refused, and he broke our engagement. That's the end of that story."

Tears brimmed in her eyes, but she went on, her voice trembling. "I made up my mind that I would protect my father, care for him, as he'd always done for me. I'd do everything within my power to keep intact the last shreds of his pride. It's all he has left."

"He has you," Vince said gently. "He has you, Katha."

"I can't turn back the clock, make him the strong, healthy man he was before the stroke. I can only love him. I put his name next to mine on the company logo as . . . I don't know . . . a statement of sorts to make him aware of how proud I am to be his daughter. I'm very protective of him, of who sees him, who knows how disabled he is. I'll never leave him as long as he's alive and needs me."

She blinked against her tears, willing them not to fall.

"So, now you know about Bobby Logan, the other half of Logan and Logan Typing Service. Jane is his nurse. She lives here because she has no family. She's wonderful with my father. She understands his pride, just as I do. Robert Logan is, will always be, the finest man I've ever known."

And Katha Logan, Vince thought, was the most incredible woman he'd ever had the honor of meeting.

Before he was aware that he'd moved, he closed the distance between them and drew her into his arms. He held her close, the feminine aroma of spring flowers filling his senses, floating over him. She felt small and fragile in his arms. She was protecting her father out of love, and he, Vince Santini, would protect *her* out of . . . Hell, he didn't know why, but that wasn't important now. What mattered was that she wasn't alone, not anymore.

Katha allowed herself to lean against Vince, to savor his strength, the power in his arms. Just for a moment, she told herself. Just for a moment she was going to allow herself to feel protected, shielded from pain, worry, reality. Just for a moment, there in the haven of Vince's embrace.

After a few minutes Katha slowly, reluctantly, eased away from him, and managed a small smile. "So, there you have it. I hope I haven't put a damper on the evening. Shall we go to dinner now?"

"Not just yet. Is my tie still straight?"

"Yes, it's fine."

"Good. I wouldn't want to meet your father with a sloppy tie. That makes a lousy first impression."

"What?"

"Hey, I'm an old-fashioned Italian boy. I'm supposed to say hello to my date's family when I pick her up. So, here I am, picking you up and ready to say hello to Robert Logan."

"Vince, you don't have to do this. I appreciate it, but it isn't necessary. Besides, this isn't even a real date. It's a charade, remember?"

"Forget that part. Do you want to go tell Jane that I'm coming in to meet your father?"

"Why are you insisting on doing this?"

"Because . . ." He hesitated, running one hand over the back of his neck. "Because I am, that's all. Go on, go ask Jane if it's okay."

"Well . . . all right." She started across the room, stopped and looked back at him, then went down the hall.

Vince squeezed the bridge of his nose, closing his eyes for a moment. Emotions were churning inside him, foreign emotions that had no names. He shook his head, trying to still the cacophony of voices in his mind.

He suddenly felt as though he'd stepped out of himself, was watching from afar, someone who was familiar, yet wasn't. He was different somehow, changed.

Dear Lord, he thought, what was happening to him? A part of him was filled with a warmth like nothing he'd ever known before. Another section of his being was consumed by a bone-chilling fear.

Fear of what? Warmth from where? Dammit, he was losing his mind. He had to figure out what was going on, what was happening to him. He had to know what Katha Logan was doing to him.

"Vince?" she said from the doorway. "You can come in now . . . if you still want to."

He nodded and crossed the room. Katha led him down the hallway where they'd gone the night he'd placed the tracing device on her modem. He realized there were three more small bedrooms in addition to the one Katha had converted into her office. She stopped at the first open doorway and looked up at him.

"Vince . . ."

"Trust me," he said, looking directly into her eyes. "Please."

She did trust him, Katha thought. She was allowing him to come inside the protective walls she'd built around her beloved father. And the walls surrounding her own heart? Was Vince slowly, but surely, chipping away at them as well? She couldn't think about that now. Not now.

"Well," a voice said, "here's Katha and her young man, Robert. Isn't it lovely to have so much company this evening?"

Katha looked at Vince for another long moment. It was a quiet moment, which held great depth and understanding. And in that moment, they were drawn even closer to each other. At last Katha was able to turn away. She entered the room with Vince right behind her.

Robert Logan, Vince instantly knew, had once been a big, robust man. The thin, pale, white-haired man in the hospital bed still had wide shoulders and large hands. The bed was in a semisitting position, the blankets pulled up to his waist. His sunken chest had probably been capable of producing a booming laugh and a rich, deep voice.

But Robert Logan now, Vince saw, was a frail entity. He leaned slightly to the right, as though lacking the strength to sit erect. The entire right side of his face was drawn downward, his eye nearly closed, his mouth at an odd, unnatural angle and partially open. His right hand was tucked beneath his blankets.

Katha moved to the head of the bed. "Dad, this is Vincent Santini. Vince, my father, Robert Logan."

Robert lifted his left hand, and Vince took it with his left, surprised to feel an amazing amount of strength in the dry, gnarled fingers.

"I'm pleased to meet you, sir," Vince said, and released Robert's hand.

"Pleased," Robert said. His speech was thick, as though cotton filled his mouth.

Vince's glance skittered over Jane. She looked like a classic grandmother: plump, with gray hair, rosy cheeks, and a bright smile.

"Going . . . out?" Robert asked. "Look . . . pretty, Katha."

"Why thank you," she said. "I bet you were beginning to think I'd forgotten how to get all gussied up. Vince and I are going to dinner."

Jane unobtrusively reached over and wiped away saliva from Robert's chin, then straightened the collar of his pajamas. She completed the procedure quickly and naturally.

"Take . . . good care . . . my baby," Robert said, directing his attention to Vince.

"You can count on it," Vince said, smiling. "Guaranteed."

Robert looked at Vince intently. Vince held the older man's gaze until Robert nodded.

"Good, good," he said.

"It's time for your medicine, Robert," Jane said, "and for you to get some sleep. I imagine these young people are eager to be on their way. We old folks need our rest. I, for one, am ready for a warm bath, then a soft pillow."

Katha leaned over and kissed her father on the cheek. "Good night, Daddy. Sleep well and remember I love you."

"Love you," Robert said. "Come . . . again, Vince. Watch . . . football."

"You're on," Vince said. "I'm always ready to see the Rams win."

"Bull," Robert said. "Rams . . . stink."

"Daddy," Katha said. "For heaven's sake."

"Oh, yeah?" Vince said. "I've got five bucks that says that the Rams will win their next game."

"Covered," Robert said.

"I'm in for five," Jane added. "The Rams are useless."

Vince nodded. "Covered. Easy money. You two better be ready to pay up."

Robert made a gurgling sound, and the left side of his mouth lifted in a smile as the chuckle surfaced.

Oh, thank you, Vince, Katha thought. Her father was laughing in his own special way, and his one green eye that still had sight was twinkling with mischief and merriment. What a warm, wonderful man, Vincent Santini was.

"Dandy," she said. "We're running a gambling parlor here." She paused. "I'll match your bets. I think the Rams are hot stuff."

Vince laughed, and Robert once again made the gurgling noise as he lifted his left hand in a thumbs-up gesture.

"Enough for tonight," Jane said. "Off with you two now."

"Good night," Katha and Vince said in unison, then started toward the door.

"Katha," Robert said.

She and Vince stopped and turned around to look at him.

"Yes?"

"Fly . . . with the . . . angels. Been too long . . . since you . . . did."

Katha blinked against sudden tears, then smiled

warmly at her father. "I will, Daddy. I'll fly with the angels."

"Good," Robert said. "Go."

The night was clear and cold, but Katha decided to wear only a whisper soft, cream-colored shawl, rather than her heavy coat. Stars twinkled like silvery Christmas lights in the heavens as she and Vince walked to his car. He helped her in, and minutes later pulled away from the curb.

"Thank you," she said quietly.

"For what?" he asked, glancing over at her.

"For being so kind to my father. For treating him as an equal. For betting five dollars with him on a football game. For making him laugh. For—for ignoring how he looks and talking to him man to man."

"Katha, he *is* a man. He's not the father you grew up with as far as outward appearance goes, but he's the same person inside. The jerk you were engaged to isn't worth wasting my breath on except to say what I just said: The guy was a jerk. You seem to be forgetting how long I've been a cop, what I've seen, where I've been. For God's sake, the sight of a man who has had a stroke isn't going to cause me to cut and run."

"I . . ."

"And another thing. You're also forgetting that my grandfather raised me. I watched him grow old, become frail, then die. It didn't lessen my love and respect for him."

"I . . ."

He shot her a quick grin. "Except for having lousy judgment about football teams, I think"—his smile faded—"that Robert Logan is one helluva fine man. So, don't thank me because it makes it sound as though I put on an act in that room. I didn't. I truly didn't, Katha."

She wanted to throw her arms around his neck and hug him. She wanted to tell him how rare and wonderful he was. She wanted him to know that her feelings for him were growing stronger with every beat of her racing heart.

But she said nothing.

"You mentioned," Vince said, "that Jane lives with you. Did she hear anything the night I was there to put the trace on?"

"No. She has one night off a week, and, fortunately, she was visiting her daughter and grandchildren that night."

Vince nodded, and they rode in silence for several minutes.

"What did your father mean," Vince asked abruptly, "about flying with angels?"

She smiled. "When I was a little girl, I asked him why angels could fly. He said it was because they were wise enough to set aside their worries and woes, their heavy, inner burdens. Ever since then, whenever my dad felt I was working too hard, or being too gloomy, or distressed, he'd tell me to fly with the angels. After all these years, his saying that makes me stop, take a breath, and settle down again with my priorities straight."

Vince nodded. "I like that. To fly with angels. That's really great. You told him that you would. So, tonight there'll be no heavy talk about the case, the welfare rolls, printouts from modems . . . none of that. Tonight, Katha Logan, you and I are going to fly with the angels."

"Perfect," she said. "Yes, that's perfect."

And it was.

Hours later as Katha lay in bed, allowing the mist of sleep to drift over her, she decided the evening with Vince had, indeed, been as close to perfection as anything could be.

The restaurant he'd chosen was expensive and beautifully decorated to create a romantic, intimate atmosphere. The food was delicious, but she'd hardly noticed. Time and again, she'd been struck by just how incredibly masculine and handsome Vince was. She'd felt lovely and special, too, as he paid rapt attention to everything she said and did.

They'd talked for hours, covering the mundane to the major; favorite books and movies, politics, the best ice cream, the merits of the Rams, and on and on.

It had been a sharing time, getting-to-know-you-so-much-better time. They had set aside the stresses and worries of everyday life, and concentrated on each other.

They had flown with the angels.

From the moment that Vince had declared that was how the evening should be, right through to the wonderful, breath-stealing kisses in her living room when he'd brought her home, it had all been perfect.

Katha drifted off to sleep, a soft smile on her lips.

Vince stood in his dark bedroom, clad only in his slacks as he stared out over the sprawling city.

He'd started to prepare for bed, then stopped, knowing he wouldn't sleep. The confusion he'd managed to push aside while with Katha had slammed against his mind again as he'd driven home. Intertwined with it was the raging hot desire that had been ignited as he'd held and kissed Katha in her living room.

He had not wanted to come home to his empty apartment and his big, empty bed. He wanted Katha Logan. He burned with the need to make love with her. After a sensational evening in her company, laughing, talking, sharing, he now felt terribly alone . . . and lonely.

"Dammit," he said, smacking the heel of one hand against the window frame.

Would making love with Katha ease the ever-increasing turmoil within him? Would the strange, new emotions fade into oblivion once his physical frustration had been satisfied?

He didn't think so.

As angry as that realization made him, he just didn't think so.

The weight of his confusion was heavy, suddenly exhausting him to the bone.

And he knew he would have to settle that confusion if he was to ever again fly with the angels. . . .

Six

"Go ahead, Vince," Tander said, "wear out my carpet. I'll just have it replaced and bill you." Tander was slouched down in a leather chair in the main lounge of his yacht, his long legs stretched out in front of him and crossed at the ankle. His fingers were laced loosely on his chest as he watched Vince trek back and forth with heavy strides. "Would it be funny if I said you were rocking the boat?"

"No."

Tander shrugged. "Then I won't bother to say it. Could you light somewhere, Santini? You're driving me nuts. I tell you over the phone that I should finish cracking the code to get into the computer program of the welfare rolls by tomorrow, then you appear on my doorstep, or yacht step, an hour later.

You've now been here for fifteen minutes, and you've done nothing but dig a trench in my floor. Vince, what is your problem?"

Vince stopped, scowled at Tander, then sat down on one of the sofas. "Nothing."

"Oh, well, I'm glad to hear that. I could have sworn you had something on your mind." He paused. "How's Katha? Let's see, you two went out to dinner the night before last. Have you talked to her since then?"

"No." Vince leaned his head back and closed his eyes. He had seen her, in dreams that caused him to sleep restlessly at night, when he managed to sleep at all. He'd wake up to find himself reaching for her across the empty bed. Dammit, he was a wreck. "No."

Tander frowned as he leaned forward, resting his elbows on his knees. "Seriously, Vince, is there something you'd like to get off your chest? You look like hell, and my beat-up carpet can give evidence to the fact that you're not in a laid-back frame of mind. To quote the ever-famous Declan Harris, you're showing signs of being stressed-out to the max."

Vince opened his eyes and stared at the ceiling for a long moment, then lifted his head to meet Tander's gaze.

"I'll work it out," he said. "There have been a lot of changes in my life lately. You know, leaving the police force, opening my own detective agency, meeting . . ." His voice trailed off.

"Katha?" Tander said quietly.

Vince's eyes narrowed with anger. Tander didn't flinch. He continued to hold Vince's gaze, his face expressionless. Vince took a deep breath, let it out slowly, and the anger dissipated as quickly as it had come.

"Katha is different," he said. Standing up, he began to pace again. "I've never known a woman like her before."

Tander nodded. "I'll go along with that. You've always dated sophisticated women, who want a lot of fun and no commitment. Katha's not like that. She's . . ."

"She's honest and sincere, and—and just so damn special. She deserves a man who can make a commitment. She's not my type, not even close." He dropped down onto the sofa again. "But . . . Oh, hell, just forget it."

"Now, in my opinion—"

"I said forget it," Vince said gruffly.

Tander held up both hands. "Okay, fine, whatever you say. We won't discuss Katha Logan."

"She brings out protective instincts in a man, you know what I mean?"

"Yep."

"She's strong, though, and is carrying a lot of responsibility. Her father . . . No, it's not my place to reveal that. She's very careful about it. He's a fine man, her father. I liked him right off. You can feel the love between Katha and Robert Logan. It's great."

"Yep."

"There's just something about Katha that's . . . Hell, she's driving me out of my mind. I thought that by not seeing her for a couple of days, I would . . . But she's taken up residency in my brain and . . . What in the hell am I going to do about her? Dammit, Tander, quit pushing me. I told you I didn't want to talk about Katha."

"Gosh, buddy, I'm sorry." Tander coughed to camouflage an uncontrollable burst of laughter. "Actually, Vince, I'm glad you came by. I was going to call you again."

"Oh?"

"I got word that there's some problems at the Alaskan oil wells I own. I have to get up there."

"Now?"

"I told them I'd be there as quickly as I could. So, new plan. I'll finish cracking that computer code by working through the night, then take off early tomorrow. I was going to search for the virus, but Katha will have to step in and do that."

"Oh, now wait a minute."

"Don't panic. She can do it from right here on the yacht. She won't have to be anywhere near the welfare department. I'll leave instructions for her, and she can have a look at it. Bring her out here tomorrow morning—you have a key—and make yourselves at home. My crew is on R and R, so no one will disturb you."

"Well . . ."

"Good. That's settled. Never buy oil wells, Vince. They're a pain in the butt." The telephone rang. Tander crossed the room and lifted the receiver. "Hello? . . . Hi, there, lovely lady. How's life? . . . Oh, yeah? I'll be damned. . . . Yep, he is . . . You bet I will, sweetheart. He'll hightail it right over there . . . Take care. 'Bye." He replaced the receiver and turned to Vince. "That was Katha."

"What? She called *you*? Why in the hell did she call *you*?"

"Good Lord, settle down, would you? She called me because she was trying to track you down."

"Why? What's wrong? What did she say?"

"Santini, shut up. You're losing it so fast, it's a crime. Katha said to tell you that she just got another message over her modem that wasn't meant for her. The printout, thanks to my nifty tracing device, shows the telephone number the call originated from."

"Holy hell," Vince said, starting toward the door.

"I'll contact you when I get back from Alaska," Tander yelled after him.

"Fine. See ya."

Tander laughed and shook his head. "You're a goner, Santini. You're down for the count, but you haven't figured it out yet." Suddenly he frowned. "Now where am I going to go? I don't own any oil wells in Alaska."

• • •

Katha stood by the front window in the living room, her arms folded tightly, a single sheet of paper clutched in one hand.

Vince was on his way to her house. In a very short time, she'd be seeing him again . . . the bum. She'd been so sure he'd come by, or call, the day after their perfect evening together, but he hadn't . . . the rat. She'd fallen off her rosy cloud with a painful thud, and realized that she'd placed far too much emphasis on those glorious hours spent with him. They certainly had meant nothing to Mr. Santini . . . the creep.

She was going to forget about their kisses, she told herself firmly, dismiss the memories of the desire that had swirled deep within her. She'd brush aside the remembrance of the feel of his muscular body when she nestled close to him. She'd chalk up as unimportant the fact that he hovered in her thoughts through the day, and followed her into her dreams at night. She'd operate on a strictly business level as he apparently intended to do . . . the louse.

She was capable—she hoped—of putting on a cool, professional front while with him. But what was she to do when she was alone? What was she to do about the frightening question that taunted her day and night?

Was she falling in love with Vincent Santini?

Could that be what was happening to her? Why didn't she know? She'd been engaged once, had been so sure she'd found the right man. But that was then, and this was now. And Vince was like no man she'd ever known. The feelings he evoked in her were those of a woman, and she now knew she'd been a child when she had believed she was in love before.

Oh, no, she thought. She couldn't fall in love with Vince.

Because he was the wrong man.

He would break her heart and walk out of her life, leaving her alone to cry.

Vince wanted no part of a serious relationship. He'd been very honest about that. She didn't necessarily agree that his work didn't blend with a commitment to a woman, but she was definitely aware that he had no intention of changing his stand on the matter.

Was she such a dimwit that she was falling in love with him anyway?

"Oh, Katha," she said aloud, "are you really that stupid?"

She stiffened when she saw his car pull up in front of the house. He got out and strode quickly toward the door.

Go away! she thought frantically, even as her heart welcomed him.

He knocked on the door. She took a deep breath before crossing the room.

Strictly business, she reminded herself. She had to protect her pride. She was Robert Logan's daughter, and she'd been taught the importance of self-pride.

She lifted her chin and opened the door.

"Hello, Vince," she said. *Hello, my love.* "You made good time getting here." *And in stealing my heart.* "Please, come in." *And then please leave soon before I fall apart. Because . . . because . . .*

She loved him.

In that fleeting second she knew. As she'd felt herself melt inside at the mere sight of him, she knew. All the glorious memories of their time together swept over her like a crashing wave, and she knew.

She was in love with Vincent Santini.

She shut the door after he stepped into the room, and prayed that no clue to her emotional turmoil was evident on her face, in her eyes, or in her voice when she spoke.

"Hello, Katha," he said, turning to face her. "Tander said you received another message over your modem."

"Yes, I did. Here." She held out the now crumbled paper.

Vince took it, smoothed it, and focused his attention on the words.

Get it together, Santini, he told himself. He mustn't think about kissing Katha, holding her close to his overheated body. *Read the damn message!* It seemed like an eternity since he'd stood there kissing Katha after their evening out. It was so damn long since he'd . . . He wanted to . . . He needed to . . .

"What do you think?" Katha asked.

That he'd totally lost his mind, he thought bleakly.

This whisper of a woman had driven him right over the edge to insanity.

He cleared his throat and forced himself to concentrate on the printout. "Let's see here. It says, 'Why no acknowledgement of message? Are you eighty-sixing this operation? Welfare rolls are at stake.' Interesting. Very interesting."

"What does it mean? I gather this person doesn't realize the other transmission went astray, and can't understand why his partner hasn't answered. But what is eighty-sixing?"

"That's street slang for getting out, leaving. It's used in different ways, but means the same thing. A guy might be eighty-sixed from a bar if he's had too much to drink and is getting rowdy."

"Oh, I see. So, he's asking his partner if he's no longer a part of the deal."

"That's how I read it. I don't know why this came over your modem, but we're lucky it did. The telephone number this originated from is right here at the top of the paper. We're about to wrap this up, Katha. I'll pull some strings, get the address for this phone number, and we'll have our boy. I'm sure he won't take the fall for this alone. He'll be hollering his partner's name before we put the cuffs on him. And that will be all she wrote on this little number."

"Well, isn't that super?" Katha said, forcing herself to smile. Then Vince would be gone, would walk out of the door and out of her life. "Yes, that's . . . splendid."

"Yeah," he said gruffly. "Who's here in the house?"

"My father is sleeping. Jane has gone to the library, and my secretary left an hour ago."

"Good. Let's go into your office so I can use the phone. A lot of cops owe me a lot of favors. I'll have one of them talk to the telephone company and get the address for this number. Then I'll decide how to handle going in after the guy."

"All right."

Vince watched her cross the room to the hall, feeling the cold knot in his gut tighten as the burning desire within him increased. He walked slowly behind her, wondering what in the hell he was going to do.

Thirty minutes later, Katha closed the drapes on the office windows as dusk gave way to darkness, then snapped on the desk lamp. Vince sat in the leather chair behind the desk, staring at the telephone as he drummed his fingers impatiently on the desktop.

They'd hardly spoken to each other since entering the room. Vince had called a police officer, made his request, and was promised a reply as quickly as possible.

Now they waited.

Katha was painfully aware of the tension building in the room. It seemed to grow with each passing second. It was, of course, nerve-racking to watch a telephone that refused to ring, but it was more than that. There was a current of sensuality weaving back and forth between her and Vince, an acute awareness that was becoming unbearable.

No, she thought, that might not be true. It could very well be that only *she* was terribly disturbed by Vince's proximity, while all his mental attention was focused on the telephone.

"There's someone coming in the front door," he said. She nearly jumped at the unexpected sound of his deep voice. "I imagine it's Jane."

"Hello, hello," a voice called. "I'm back."

"Yes, that's Jane," Katha said. "I'll go tell her that you're here, and let her know that my father was still sleeping when I last checked on him."

Vince leaned back in the chair as she left the room, and let out the pent-up breath he felt he'd been holding for a year.

Lord, he thought, he was so wired, he was going to blow a fuse in his brain. He was, he hoped, giving Katha the impression that he was Mr. Super P. I., his concentration centered on the telephone and the plan of action he'd put into motion once he received the address.

What a joke, he thought dryly. When he got the address, he'd somehow force himself to get into his detective mode so he didn't screw up. But in the meantime, all he could think about was Katha.

He got to his feet and went to the doorway of the office, hearing the murmur of voices in the distance. He dragged a restless hand through his hair, then turned and walked to one of the windows, parting the drapes and looking out into the darkness.

Katha certainly seemed calm, cool, and collected, he thought sullenly. It apparently hadn't bothered her one whit that he hadn't called or come by since their special evening together. Hadn't that night meant anything to her? Maybe not. Maybe he was the only one who was an emotional basket case.

Well, great, he fumed. He was being turned inside out and backward by her image and the memories of being with her, while she went blissfully about her business without a care in the world. She sure as hell didn't give the impression that she was tied up in knots over *him*. Thanks a whole helluva lot, Katha Logan.

"Vince?" she said, coming back into the room. "Jane is going to eat dinner with my father now. There's a pot of homemade soup simmering on the stove. We can have some whenever we're ready."

He dropped the drape back into place and turned to her. "I'm not hungry."

She shrugged. "Okay. I just thought I'd let you know that the soup is there. It's not important."

He closed the distance between them in three long strides and gripped her shoulders. "What is important, Katha? Why don't you clue me in? Just what in the hell *is* important to you?"

Her eyes widened. "What? I don't understand what—"

"Damn you," he muttered, and brought his mouth down hard on hers.

Katha's body went stiff as a board from the shock of Vince's unexpected words and actions. In the next instant, as the rough onslaught of his mouth gentled, she raised her arms to encircle his neck and her eyes drifted closed. She parted her lips to receive his questing tongue, and fit her body against his as he drew her to him.

This was Vince, she thought happily as she returned his kiss in total abandon. And she loved him. Was this the last kiss they would ever share, the end of the heaven of being in his strong embrace? Was this the end, and thus the beginning of her heartache, loneliness, and tears? Oh, no, not yet. It mustn't be over this soon. But why did Vince seem so angry, so . . .

Rational thought fled as the kiss deepened. Vince slid his hands down her back to the slope of her buttocks, nestling her to the cradle of his hips. His arousal pressed against her; full, heavy, bold evidence of his desire for her.

And she wanted him, Katha thought hazily. She wanted to make love with Vincent Santini because she was *in* love with him. It was right, the way it should be. The way it *would* be . . . before he left her.

The blood pounded through Vince's veins as his desire grew, the fire of passion raging within him. He heard a groan, dimly realized it had come from him, and swept his hands over her body as his tongue danced with hers.

He wanted this woman! And *she* wanted *him*. He could feel her surrendering to him, giving herself, her lips, her entire body, telling him she was his for the taking. He would have her and end the aching agony of his arousal. Guilt would not gnaw at him later because Katha was letting him know she wanted him.

Why? he wondered. Why did she want him? Was it simply lust, a purely physical response to his seduction of her? Did her heart feel the same way as her body? But what in the hell difference did it make? It didn't matter.

Yes, it did. Dammit, it did.

He lifted his head and released her, stepping back. She staggered slightly and opened her eyes to meet his smoldering gaze.

"I want you, Katha," he said, his voice husky with passion.

"Yes," she whispered. "I want you, too, Vince."

"Why?"

Katha blinked, willing the trembling within her to quiet. "Why?"

"It's a reasonable question. Why do you want to make love with me?"

Because I'm *in* love with you, you dolt, she thought. Oh, Lord, she'd never forgive herself if she said those words, destroyed her last shred of pride.

"A more approriate 'why,' " she said, straightening her shoulders, "would be, why are you so angry, and—and why are you insisting that I answer a question that isn't, in my opinion, reasonable at all?"

"The hell it isn't!"

"All right, Mr. Santini, then you answer it. Why do *you* want to make love with *me*?"

"Because I . . ." He stopped. Because he burned with the need of her. Because the turmoil and confusion churning within him was eating him alive. Because he'd never been through a living hell like this before, and he had to break the spell, the hold, that Katha had on him. And he had no intention of saying any of that to her. "Forget it. I want you, you want me, that's clear enough."

"Oh? What happened to your reasonable question of 'why,' Vince?"

"I said forget it," he repeated loudly.

The telephone rang.

"Well, well," Katha said, glaring at him, "just like in the movies . . . saved by the bell."

He shot her a dark look, then snatched up the receiver. "Logan residence . . . Yes, it's Santini. Go ahead." He sat down behind the desk and scribbled something on a piece of paper. "Hell, that's as lousy as it can get. You're sure? . . . All right. Thanks for your help." He dropped the receiver back into place and muttered several earthy expletives.

"What's wrong?" Katha asked.

"The call came from a phone booth in the warehouse district. In other words, we have nothing."

"That doesn't make sense. The person expected an answer, so he has to have a computer modem setup. He's transmitting his messages through the wrong modem—mine—but it indicates that these people have sophisticated equipment."

"That may be true, but this particular call came from a phone booth." He smacked the desktop with the palm of his hand. "Dammit, we're back to square one. I'll drive down to the warehouse district and look around, but this joker is long gone, you can bet on it."

"So now what?"

Vince got to his feet. "Tander is cracking the code to get into the computer at the welfare department. He was going to search for the virus, but he has an emergency in Alaska." He paused. "I didn't know he owned any oil wells. Anyway, can you clear the decks here so you can be free tomorrow?"

"Yes, but . . ."

"We'll go to Tander's yacht, and you can look for the virus, using his computer equipment. I thought we'd have this guy in the can tonight, and he could tell us where the virus was but . . . Damn. I'll pick you up at seven tomorrow morning. Tander's crew is away so we won't be disturbed, and you won't be anywhere near the welfare department. It's perfectly safe."

Oh, ha! Katha thought. Being alone with Vince on a luxurious yacht was not her idea of safe. After the kiss they shared, and the avenue her mind had traveled during it, even with her father and Jane right down the hall . . . No, there was nothing safe about Tander's yacht. The whole scenario shouted "Danger!"

And the really depressing part was that she was more afraid of herself and what she might do than she was of Vince.

"Katha?"

"What? Oh, yes, fine. I'll be ready to go at seven tomorrow."

"Good. I'll say hello to your father and head down to the warehouse district." He paused again, then came from behind the desk to stand in front of her. "Katha, I . . . Look, I'm sorry about what happened a few minutes ago. I'm tired, and I guess my temper is on a raw edge. That's no excuse for taking it out on you, and I apologize. I really am sorry, Katha."

"For what?" she asked quietly. "Kissing me? Are you sorry you kissed me, Vince?"

He drew one thumb over her lips. "No. That isn't what I meant, and I think you know that. Kissing you, holding and touching you is . . ." His gaze slid to her parted lips, then back to her eyes. "I'd better get out of here. I'll see you in the morning."

Katha nodded, but didn't move as Vince left the office. Proper manners, she knew, dictated that she accompany him to her father's room, then see him to the door. But she couldn't, not now, not while her throat was aching with unshed tears.

She was certain Vince's feelings for her were growing, and he was angry because of it. His stand on having no serious relationships was firmly in place. He was fighting his own emotions and he would win, because he was strong, stronger than she. She had lost her emotional battle, and fallen in love with him.

How nice it would be, she mused, to set aside her inner anguish for a few stolen hours and fly with the angels, free of worries and woes. But she couldn't, for the bleak picture of her future was too heavy to lift away temporarily so she could soar with a light heart.

She snapped off the lamp on the desk, dropping a curtain of darkness over the office. Lights shone down the hall, and she heard Jane's cheerful laughter in the distance.

But Katha was alone. There in the dark room, she could still smell the lingering scent of Vince's masculine aroma, still feel his presence, hear his voice echoing in the silence. She would see him tomorrow. It wasn't quite over, but she missed him already as she envisioned the last goodbye that was soon to come.

A single tear slid down her cheek.

Seven

The next morning Katha dressed in jeans and a bright blue sweater. The cheerful color was at the opposite end of the spectrum from her gloomy mood.

She would not, she promised herself, give Vince any clue that she was totally miserable. Her Logan pride would, she hoped, hold her in good stead.

As she sipped a mug of tea at the kitchen table, she told herself to shift her mental attention to the task she faced that day. There was a tremendous challenge awaiting her as she attempted to find the virus hidden in the welfare rolls' computer program. While on Tander's yacht, she would be drawing on her intelligence and the extensive training in computers she'd had in college. It was rather exciting to realize it was now up to her to stop this nefarious crime.

What if, she thought suddenly, Tander was right and there wasn't any nefarious crime? What if the whole shebang was nothing more than kids playing games back and forth between their computers?

No, she reasoned, Vince was a seasoned police officer. He was a top-notch detective, who could recognize a crime in progress. He hadn't worn his gun and badge for all those years for nothing.

The previous night she'd explained to her father and Jane that she would be leaving in the early morning with Vince. He needed her assistance in a complicated computer matter, she'd said, and she wasn't certain what time she'd be back. The fact that her audience had given her knowing smiles indicated she had blithered on at top speed during her explanation.

She rinsed out her mug, set it in the dish drainer, and went into the living room just as a soft knock sounded at the front door. She ignored the increased tempo of her heart, forced a phony smile onto her face, and opened the door.

"Hello, Katha," Vince said. "Are you ready to go?"

She looked at the center of his chest, which was covered by a white sweater. "Yes, all set. Just let me get my purse."

A few moments later she stepped out onto the

porch, closed the door behind her, and breezed past Vince with an inane comment about the lovely, brisk morning air. She got into his car and busied herself picking imaginary lint from her jeans.

Vince walked slowly toward the car, his eyes narrowed. Was Katha acting strangely? he wondered. She was bright and bouncy, but she hadn't looked directly at him. Unless she had a fetish for white sweaters, she had purposely avoided meeting his gaze.

Not that he blamed her for being wary around him, he admitted. His behavior the night before had not been a class act, and he was in no better mental shape today. He'd spent another restless night, and awakened with a pounding headache.

But he'd vowed as he'd consumed three steaming cups of bitter black coffee, that he'd somehow set aside his confusion while with Katha today, and conduct himself in a professional manner. He'd be one hundred percent hard-core private investigator. He'd be who he was before he met Katha—a detective, a man, alone.

The drive to the marina was made in total silence.

Tander's yacht gleamed in the morning sunlight, its brass railings sparkling. As Katha stepped onto the deck she felt, once again, as though she were being transported to another world. This was how that elusive "other half" lived. This was the toy of a jet-setter. This was a place where Vince was comortable. This was where games might be played by rules she didn't understand.

Vince unlocked a door, then stepped back for her to proceed him. They went down the stairs, and Vince nodded in the opposite direction from the main lounge. Farther alone the corridor, he opened another door.

"Oh, good heavens," Katha said as she entered the room, "look at all this equipment."

Vince glanced around the large room. It's only furniture were a few chairs and several long tables. Each table supported various computers and other sophisticated machines.

"Tander's really into computers," he said. "He has a natural aptitude for them, and once he sets his mind to doing something, he doesn't give up until he's accomplished his goal."

Just like Vince, Katha thought. Vince was as stubborn as Tander. But while Tander's energies had been centered on cracking the code to the welfare program, Vince was zeroed in on smothering, or ignoring, his feelings for her. Drat the man. She was in love with him, wanted to spend the rest of her life with him, have his baby, be his partner, his best friend.

Katha, remember your pride.

"Well, I'd better get started," she said brightly. "Let's see now. Tander must have left me some instructions. Now, if I were Tander where would I leave a note?"

"Katha . . ." Vince frowned and shook his head. He picked up a manilla folder from a table. "Here, this has your name on it."

"Oh, good, thank you." She opened the folder and began to read.

Dammit, Vince thought, she *still* hadn't looked at him. Well, fine. It made his vow not to touch her a lot easier if she didn't gaze at him with those beautiful green eyes of hers. His libido would be easier to control if he didn't gaze at her soft, kissable lips and remember what it had been like to—Cool it, Santini. Just knock it off.

"That's the computer I'm to use," Katha said, crossing the room. She settled in the chair in front of the machine. "According to this report of Tander's, he found three separate programs in the welfare computer. One is to print the checks. The second is to print the envelopes for the checks. The third is to print the envelopes for the food vouchers that come into the department each month."

"Food vouchers?" Vince asked.

"Yes. The vouchers vary month to month, apparently, depending on the surplus available from the big companies. You know, dairy products, bread, pastries, fruits and vegetables, things like that. Tander says here that there are outlets all over the city. The people take the voucher to the store shown on their coupon, and get what they've been chosen to receive that month."

"We're not interested in that," Vince said. "Concentrate on the program that prints the envelopes for the checks."

Katha glared at him over her shoulder. "I realize that, Vince." She redirected her attention to the folder. "I'm sorry. I shouldn't have snapped at you."

He shoved his hands into his back pockets and slowly crossed the room to stand next to her. "You had every right to," he said. He wanted *needed*, her to look at him. It was suddenly very important. "I realize you're intelligent enough to know which program to work on."

He felt strange, he thought. He felt . . . lonely. The invisible wall surrounding Katha was higher and stronger than ever, and he didn't know what to say to gain entrance to the inner haven, to her warmth.

"I'll . . . um . . ." He cleared his throat. "I'll go make a pot of coffee."

"All right. I'll get started here." Katha laughed. "If I can get up enough nerve to turn this thing on."

Still smiling, she looked up at him.

Their eyes met, and everything stopped. Except for the rapid beating of Katha's heart and the heated blood that pounded through Vince's veins.

Dear God, he thought as a trickle of sweat ran down his back. He loved her!

The eternal confusion in his mind faded, replaced by a message that was as clear as bright sunshine on a summer's day.

He was in love with Katha Logan.

That was what it all had meant, he thought. That was where the unfamiliar path crowded with un- named emotions had been leading him. He had been falling in love with Katha.

How had this happened? Long ago he'd made the decision never to love, not to attempt the foolish and hopeless task of combining his career with a serious relationship. He'd held true to his convictions for all that time, all those women, all those years. Until now. Until Katha. Dammit, how had this happened?

It didn't matter how it had happened, his heart answered. All that was important was that he was looking at the woman, the only woman, he'd ever loved.

What was he going to do?

"Coffee," he said, his voice rough. "I'm going to go make some coffee." He turned and strode from the room.

Katha blinked, her smile gone as she drew much needed air into her lungs. She looked at the door- way Vince had vanished through, then shifted to face the computer.

Only moments had passed, she was sure, but it had seemed as if time had been suspended when she'd met Vince's gaze. There had been no com- puter, no yacht, nothing . . . but Vince. Oh, how she loved him. And, oh, how she wished she didn't. By being weak, by not gaining control of her emotions early on, she'd sentenced herself to loneliness and heartache.

"Oh, damn, damn," she said, then sniffled. "Stop it, Katha, and turn on the dumb machine."

She pressed a button and jumped as the computer buzzed and the green screen came alive. Lines of symbols flashed one after the next, then disappeared. The word "Hello" settled onto the center of the screen.

"Don't be cheerful," she said to the computer, then buried her nose in the folder to study the instructions Tander had given her.

Vince stood watching the dark liquid drip into the glass pot of the coffee maker. A growing pain in his hands made him realize he was gripping the edge of the counter so tightly, his knuckles were white. He released his hold and dragged both hands down his face.

He was shaken to the core and hated it. The great Vince Santini, tough cop Vincent, was falling apart. Macho Vince, who had gone up against hardened criminals, vicious thugs, and had won by both brute strength and cunning, had been cut down by a woman who probably didn't weigh more than a hundred and ten pounds.

Now what? he asked himself. Now . . . nothing. He wouldn't allow himself to go further. Katha must never know the depth of his feelings for her. He was still a detective, things hadn't changed. Love and commitment weren't in the cards for him. He'd seen too many cops' lives shattered by marriages that failed, that couldn't survive the crushing weight of a police officer's career.

When this case was wrapped up, he would walk away from Katha. He'd never see her again, never hold, kiss, touch her again. He'd spend the remainder of his days as he'd always been, alone.

And the image of a future without Katha was chilling. So empty, cold, and so damn lonely.

He poured himself a mug of the now brewed coffee and leaned against the counter as he took a sip.

He knew he was postponing returning to the room where Katha was working. He wasn't ready to see her yet. She was the woman he loved. He loved her. He'd fallen in love with her. No matter how he rearranged the words, it was still unbelievable. How in heaven's name had this happened?

And furthermore, he was such a jerk that he'd fallen in love with a woman who didn't love *him*. Not that it mattered because he had no intention of pursuing the whole mess, but still . . .

Katha cared for him, of that he was certain. It was evident each time he took her into his arms and kissed her. She'd said she wanted him, wanted to make love with him, but she'd never said she was in love with him. It was no big deal, of course, because he wasn't going to tell her that *he* loved *her*, but still . . .

Muttering a variety of expletives in English and Italian, Vince topped off his coffee, filled another mug for Katha, and placed both on a tray. He found a package of sugar cookies in the cupboard and tossed it onto the tray.

He'd probably slosh coffee all over the cookies, he thought, as he picked up the tray and left the room. The way his life was going, he didn't seem capable of doing anything right.

At the doorway to the computer room, he stopped. Katha's back was to him, and she was leaning forward, concentrating on the lines of symbols that covered the computer screen.

His heart thudded wildly and heat gathered low in his body. He loved that woman, he thought incredulously. Beautiful Katha, with her silky auburn curls and dusting of freckles on her nose, her slender body that fit perfectly against him, her soft, sweet lips, had stolen his heart.

And he wanted it back!

That was good, he thought dryly. Up against the wall, Katha. Don't move until you give me back my heart.

Vince shook his head in self-disgust, then crossed the room and placed the tray next to the computer.

"Coffee and cookies," he said.

" 'Kay," she said, her gaze riveted on the computer screen. "Thanks."

He picked up his mug and moved behind her. His glance flickered over the screen and the rows of symbols he couldn't even begin to decipher, then skimmed along Katha, from the top of her head to her jean-clad bottom. Of its own volition it seemed, his free hand reached out toward her silken curls.

He stiffened and snatched his hand back, then spun around, nearly spilling his coffee. He chose one of the easy chairs onto the far side of the room and settled into it. Wrapping his hands around the mug and resting his elbows on the arms of the chair, he stared at Katha. A deep frown knitted his brows.

He wasn't going to think, he told himself. *Lord, how he loved her.* No, forget it. He was blanking his mind of all thoughts of Katha. *It was just unbelievable how much he loved, wanted, needed that woman.* Football. He'd focus on the Rams. They were a great team, a tough team, a team to be reckoned with, despite what Robert Logan said. Robert Logan was Katha's father. *And Katha was the special, wonderful, beautiful woman he loved.*

He thumped his mug down on the table next to his chair and laced his fingers on his chest. The only sound in the room was the steady, slow clicking of the computer key that Katha pressed to scroll the lines of the program upward.

Vince yawned and felt some of the tension in his body begin to ebb, then closed his eyes. The insistent thoughts and images of Katha began to blur as his series of near sleepless nights demanded their due.

He drifted off to sleep.

•   •   •

"Oh!"

Vince jerked awake, lunged to his feet, and started to reach for his gun. He staggered, blinked, then realized where he was.

"What's wrong, Katha?" he asked, his voice husky with sleep.

She stood and pushed her fists into the small of her back. "I'm stiff. I haven't moved in three hours."

"Three . . ." He looked at his watch. "Lord, I really zonked out."

She turned to face him, smiling. "I know. You were dead to the world. I can attest to the fact that you don't snore."

"That's comforting," he said, matching her smile. 'A guy worries about that, you know . . . whether or not he sounds like a dying cow when he's sleeping."

Katha rotated her neck back and forth. "Nope. You were as peaceful as a baby."

He crossed the room to stand behind her, then placed his hands on her shoulders near her neck.

"What . . ."

"Let me massage these muscles. You should have taken a break, Katha." Gently, Santini. He mustn't hurt her. She was so small and delicate. When he made love with her, he'd be so careful and—No! "Have you had any luck with the program yet?"

"No," she said, her eyes half-closed. "Oh, that feels marvelous." Such strong hands he had, but he was tempering his strength with infinite gentleness, just as he did when he held and kissed her. And just as he would when they made love. No! "I've been through the program three times, Vince. Once I learned how to read it, it was very clear. It's not complicated because it performs a simple function. There's a reason, a purpose, for every symbol that's there."

"I see," he said, continuing to massage her shoulders.

"I'll keep looking." The heat from Vince's hands was swirling lower, causing her breasts to become heavy and sensitive, aching for a soothing touch. And lower . . . deep within her, pulsing with the same steady rhythm of his fingers on her shoulders. "I'll get back to work now."

"No, relax a bit."

"But . . ." She turned to look up at him. His hands lifted with the motion, then settled again on her shoulders. She hadn't realized she'd be this close to him when she'd shifted to face him. So close, so very close.

She wanted to slide her hands up his chest, feel the soft material of his sweater and the taut muscles beneath. She wanted to nestle her body to his, to part her lips to receive his kiss, his tongue. She wanted to make love with Vince Santini. "Vince, I . . ." Her voice trailed off.

His fingers tightened on her shoulders as he looked directly into her eyes. Eyes, he realized, that were radiating the message of desire. His heart beat hard as passion swept through him, overwhelming him.

Move away from her! his mind demanded.

Not a chance, his heart answered.

Don't do it, Santini, his mind warned.

Go to hell, his heart said.

"Katha," he murmured with a groan that seemed to come from his very soul.

He lowered his head and kissed her.

As their lips met and their tongues touched, they were lost, swept away by the tide of passion that had been building within them for so long. Katha raised her arms to encircle his neck, as his hands moved to her back to draw her to him. A soft sob caught in her throat.

The kiss intensified. He gave, she received. She gave, he received. It was hunger and heat, want and need. It was Katha and Vince loving, but not saying the words. Katha and Vince wanting, their bodies speaking for them. Katha and Vince knowing that the time had come, the time to fly with the angels.

"I want you, Katha," Vince said against her lips. "I want to make love to you, with you."

"Yes," she whispered.

"Listen to me. Please, Katha, you've got to be sure this is right for you. I couldn't handle it if you were sorry, regretted it later. I'll leave you alone, go back over to that chair, and not touch you. I have to know that you want this as much as I do. It's so . . . It's just so damn important."

Oh, Vince, she thought. He was rendering himself

totally vulnerable, exposing his pride that could be shattered by her refusal to become one with him. How difficult that must be for a man like him, an incredibly strong man who held such tight control over himself and his emotions. What a precious treasure he was placing in her hands.

And what of *her* pride? she asked herself. Would making love with Vince snatch it from her, rip it to shreds? No. Their joining would be separate and apart from the declaration of love that would remain safely tucked away in her heart.

"Katha?"

"I want to make love with you, Vince. I promise you that I won't be sorry. It's right, it's good, and it's time. I know that. I know that, Vincent."

His mouth melted over hers, and his tongue delved deeply inside to find and stroke hers. A mist of sensuality seemed to swirl around them, encasing them in a sensuous cocoon where nothing could intrude. There was just the two of them, the world beyond forgotten.

Vince raised his head, then in the next instant lifted Katha into his arms. She tightly gripped his neck, inhaling his aroma, savoring his heat and strength. He carried her down the corridor and into a large bedroom. He set her on her feet next to a king-size bed and claimed her mouth once more.

In a haze of passion, Katha was vaguely aware that he was removing her clothes, then his own. He swept back the blankets on the bed, and placed her on the cool pale blue sheets.

"Katha," he said, his voice raspy. He stood beside the bed, towering above her. "Katha, please say it again. Tell me this is what you want."

With effort, she pulled herself back to reality. Her gaze slid over him, and her breath caught. He was magnificent. His body was beautiful, powerful.

Curly dark hair covered his muscled chest, then narrowed down on his flat belly. And lower yet was the very essence of his masculinity, the bold evidence of his desire for her and of all he would bring to her.

A soft smile touched her lips, and she raised her arms to welcome him. She felt no trepidation, because this was Vince. She loved him.

Vince closed his eyes for a moment to gather his control, then stretched out next to her. One hand on her stomach, he kissed her lips, her cheeks, then trailed nibbling kisses along her neck. Slowly, slowly, he moved on, across the tops of her breasts. Katha trembled.

"Beautiful," he murmured. "You're so beautiful."

His mouth closed over one taut nipple, and he laved it with his tongue before drawing it deeper into his mouth, sucking, pulling.

A purr of pleasure escaped from Katha's lips. Never before had she felt like this—aching with sweet pain, burning with exquisite heat, pulsing with raging desire. She sank her fingers into Vince's thick hair, urging him on, pressing his mouth harder onto her soft flesh.

His arousal was heavy against her as his hand skimmed over the dewy skin of her thighs, coming to rest on the auburn nest that covered her femininity.

"Oh, Vince," she said, her voice sounding strange to her own ears. "I feel so . . . Please. I want you, I need you. Now."

He moved over her, catching his weight on his forearms as he kissed her. He raised his head to meet her gaze, his muscles quivering from restraint, his body glistening with perspiration.

"Come to me," she said. *I love you, Vince.*

"Yes," he said. *Katha, I love you.*

He entered her, pressing into her gently, watching her face for any flicker of pain or fear. He saw none. She wrapped her arms around his back, holding him tightly as if to never again let him go. He thrust farther into her, gritting his teeth to retain control, and filled her with all that he was.

"Yes," Katha whispered on a little puff of air. "Oh, yes."

He began the dance of love, moving slowly inside her, then more swiftly as she lifted her hips to meet him. He drove deeper, harder, thundering within her, as all caution fled and he gave way to the passion that consumed him.

"Fly . . . with me . . . Katha, and with . . . the angels."

"The . . . angels. Yes. Oh, Vince!"

"Yes, that's it, that's it."

Rippling spasms coursed through Katha, and she tightened her hold on Vince as she teetered on the edge of an unknown abyss. She felt her body tighten around him, pulling him deeper into her. Then she was swept into oblivion, soaring in an ecstasy she'd never experienced before.

"Vincent!"

"Ah, Katha!"

He flung his head back and groaned in pure male pleasure as he found his release, joining her in that rapturous place as he shuddered, spilling his life's force into her, flying with her and the angels.

He collapsed against her, spent, his breathing labored. She clung to him, feeling his heart beating rapidly against hers. They hovered with the angels, then drifted slowly back to where it had all begun.

Vince pushed himself up onto his forearms again. "Thank you," he said quietly.

Tears clouded Katha's eyes, and her heart nearly burst with love. Such simple words, she thought, but said so sincerely, so reverently, as though she'd given him the most precious gift he'd ever received.

"No, Vince, thank *you*," she said. "I've never experienced anything so incredibly beautiful. I didn't know it could be like that. We flew, didn't we, with the angels?"

He smiled. "We certainly did." His smile faded. "It was . . . very special, Katha. Very, very special."

"Yes."

He kissed her deeply, then moved off her, pulling the blankets up to cover their cooling bodies. She snuggled close to him, one hand spread on his moist chest.

"The computer program. I should—"

"Later," he interrupted. He rested his lips lightly on her temple. "You can work on it later."

She sighed in contentment.

With their heads close together on the same pillow, they slept.

Eight

Katha awoke to the sound of rain beating against the windows and thunder rumbling in the distance. The room was in semidarkness, and she blinked several times before she realized where she was.

As the fogginess of sleep dissipated, she turned her head and frowned when she saw the bed was empty. In the next instant, she snapped her head around to look at the clock on the nightstand.

Three o'clock? In the afternoon? Yes, she supposed so. The shadowy light in the room was due to the storm, not because it was three o'clock in the morning. She'd had quite a nap, and her rumbling stomach was announcing that she was hungry.

Nice try, Miss Logan, she thought dryly. She'd mentally discussed the weather, the time of day, and the grumbling complaints of her empty stomach. She'd skittered around the major issue at hand, and that was enough dillydallying. So, okay, she was ready to get in touch with herself.

She'd made love with Vince Santini.

No, she decided, there was more to it than that.

She'd made love with Vince Santini, the man she loved with every breath in her body.

Where was the rush of guilt? she wondered. Where was the "Oh-what-have-I-done?" Where were the tears of remorse at taking such a momentous step with Vince, knowing there was no hope of a future with him?

She shifted on the bed, and her eyes widened as she became aware of a soreness in foreign places. But then she smiled, a soft smile, a womanly smile, a smile born from having shared exquisite lovemaking with the man of her heart.

There would be no guilt or tears, she realized. Among her memories when Vince left her would be the precious remembrance of becoming one with him, of flying with the angels with him.

Speaking of the man in question, she thought, where was he? Even more, what was he thinking? What would he say and do when he saw her?

She frowned, decided she'd prefer to go back to sleep and postpone seeing Vince, then called herself six kinds of coward. She flipped away the blankets and started toward the shower. The yacht was rocking as the rain and wind raged with Nature's fury.

She went into the large bathroom and closed the door.

Vince entered the bedroom carrying a tray and stopped when he saw the vacant bed. He glanced at the bathroom door as he heard the sound of the running water, then placed the tray on the nightstand. Turning on the lamp, he sat down on the bed, his gaze riveted on the closed bathroom door.

Katha was in there, he thought. Katha was awake, and thinking. He'd only dozed, thanks to his nap in the computer room, then laid next to Katha, watching her sleep. When heated desire had caused him to become uncomfortably aroused, he'd left the bed, and showered and dressed. What he hadn't done, for as long as he could delay it, was think.

But as he'd made sandwiches, his mind had demanded his attention. He was, he knew, a walking contradiction. A part of him was awed, virtually stunned, by the beautiful and emotionally moving lovemaking he'd shared with Katha. It had been so much more than the physical gratification he usually experienced. It was as though his very soul had been touched as he'd meshed his body with Katha's.

He rubbed one hand across the back of his neck. There was a flip side to the coin. He was in love with Katha, yet didn't want to be in love with her, and he had no idea what to do next.

"Damn," he said.

The water in the shower stopped, and he stiffened. Any minute now, Katha was going to come back into the bedroom. What should he say to her, what should he do? He'd never been in a situation like this before, because he'd never been in love before. To declare that love would serve no purpose as he had no intention of pursuing it further. So, what did he say? "Thanks for the toss in the hay, babycakes"? Oh, Lord.

The bathroom door opened and every muscle in Vince's body tensed as Katha emerged with a large blue towel wrapped around her. His heart thundered, and the now very familiar heat coiled deep within him.

"Oh," she said, stopping when she saw him. "I . . . Well . . . Oh."

"I brought some sandwiches and milk." He got to his feet. "Katha . . . are you all right? I mean, I didn't hurt you or . . . That is . . ." Hell, he was blowing this completely. He sounded cold and clinical, like a doctor asking for an update on a patient's condition. What about her mind? Was she sorry they'd made love? Had she cried while she'd been alone? "Dammit, are you okay?"

Katha blinked in surprise at Vince's sudden coldness. Why was he being so clinical? What was his problem? He'd been so insistent that she tell him that she wouldn't regret what they shared. It appeared Mr. Santini should have asked himself the same question before they'd proceeded to—to do what they'd proceeded to do.

"I'm fine, thank you," she said stiffly. "Why wouldn't I be? Surely you're aware of the fact that you didn't hurt me."

"Right, right." He dragged a hand through his hair. "But what about . . . you know, your mind, your emotions?" Dammit to hell! He sounded like a total jerk. He wanted to take her in his arms, pull away that towel, and make sweet love to her for hours. So why did he sound like a cop grilling a suspect in a crime?

He was regretting their lovemaking, Katha thought, feeling tears burning at the back of her eyes. He was so tense, and was probably afraid she was going to dissolve into a weeping heap, or worse yet, fling herself into his arms and declare her undying love for him. Well, ha!

She lifted her chin. "Vincent, I assured you I would feel no regret or guilt at making love with you, and I don't. What we shared was very . . . nice."

Nice! Vince's mind yelled. They'd experienced the most beautiful, fantastic, incredible lovemaking of the century, and she was calling it nice? That was all it had meant to her?

He folded his arms over his chest and narrowed his eyes. "Nice," he repeated, a muscle jumping in his tightly clenched jaw. "Okay, that's clear enough, I guess."

"Yes, I'd say that things are very clear," she said,

hoping her voice hadn't trembled. She scooped up her clothes from the floor, gripping the towel with one hand. "If you'll excuse me, I'll get dressed." She hurried back into the bathroom and closed the door.

His heart hurt, Vince thought, pressing one hand against his chest. Katha's blasé attitude about their lovemaking was causing an actual physical pain in his heart. He didn't want her to be sorry. He didn't want her to cry. But he sure as hell hadn't expected her to dust the whole thing off as—as nice. Dammit, he loved her! Of course, she didn't know that but . . .

"Scrambled eggs," he said, stalking across the room. "My brain is as mushy as scrambled eggs." He left the bedroom, closing the door behind him with more force than was necessary.

When Katha emerged from the bathroom to find Vince gone, she felt a confusing mixture of relief and disappointment.

Her logical side was glad he wasn't there to exhibit further evidence that he was sorry they'd become lovers. The purely feminine portion of her wanted him to have been waiting for her, to tell her she'd misinterpreted his words and actions, then sweep her into his arms and carry her to the bed where he'd . . .

"Shh," she said, flapping her hands in the air. "Katha, just shh."

She plunked down on the edge of the bed and

picked up one of the sandwiches from the tray. She took a bite, decided it was the worst peanut butter and jelly sandwich she'd ever tasted, and followed it with a swallow of lukewarm milk.

Her gaze slid over the tangled sheets. Vivid pictures of their lovemaking danced before her eyes, and the desire that instantly pulsed deep within her flushed her cheeks.

She took a huge bite of the sandwich, and sighed.

She deserved to sigh, she reasoned. She'd earned the right to execute one long, sad sigh, but that was all she'd allow herself.

If Mr. Santini wanted to storm around like a spoiled child because of what they'd shared, that was his problem. His attitude would not make her wish she could turn back the clock and erase the beautiful lovemaking they'd experienced together. Her pride, though cracked by Vince's rotten mood, wasn't shattered. She'd ignore him and his surly disposition, and hug the memories of their joining to her heart, mind, and soul.

She resolutely finished the sandwich and milk, thudded the glass back onto the tray, and got to her feet. With her shoulders squared and her nose tilted in the air, she crossed the room. At the door she hesitated, looked back at the bed, then turned and hurried from the room.

Vince slouched lower in the chair in the computer

room, then shifted until his gun wasn't poking him in the back. He folded his arms over his chest and stared at the tip of one shoe.

Did he look like a pouting kid? he wondered. Hell, he didn't care if he did. He was a wreck, a complete mental mess. He shouldn't have touched Katha, shouldn't have let things go as far as they had. He shouldn't have made love with her, even though he was in love with her.

Oh, hell, he thought dismally, who was he kidding? Given the chance to step back in time to that moment of decision, he'd do it all again. He'd learned with Katha the incredible difference between truly making love and just having sex. He would never forget what they'd shared. And when he left her at the end of this welfare case, as he knew he must do, he would never forget *her* either.

She sailed into the room, and he sat up abruptly.

"Time to get back to work," she said in a sing-songy voice. "Time and crime wait for no man . . . woman . . . whatever."

"Mmm," he said crossly.

She flashed him a dazzling smile, then settled into the chair in front of the computer. The steady clicking from the key she pressed accompanied the sound of the rain beating wildly against the yacht.

Vince narrowed his eyes as he looked at her. He'd like to wring her neck for being so damn cheerful, and for her "our lovemaking was very nice" spiel. No, he didn't want to wring her neck, he wanted to make love to her again, right now, with the rain as a symphony of their own private music. He wanted to kiss and touch every inch of her soft, dewy skin, hear her purrs of pleasure, feel her delicate hands on his body, savor her taste, and . . .

Okay, that's all, he told himself, as he felt his body tighten and his manhood stir. The pain in his heart was bad enough, without living with an ache in other regions of his body.

He pushed himself to his feet. "I'm going to go tune into the weather channel on the shortwave radio."

" 'Kay." Katha waggled her fingers in the air, but kept her gaze fixed on the computer screen.

Vince strode from the room, and Katha's shoulders immediately slumped. She drew in a wobbly breath as she angrily blinked away unwelcome tears. She could handle this, she told herself.

She shoved the image of Vince into a dusty corner of her brain and concentrated on the symbols of the program on the green screen.

Over two hours later, Vince reentered the computer room. "Katha?"

"Yes?" she said, not looking at him.

"I've been listening to the weather channel on the shortwave radio all this time."

"Oh. Well, I suppose weather is interesting if you

happen to be heavily into weather." She pressed a key on the computer.

"Could you pay attention for a second?" he asked, planting his hands on his hips.

"I *am* paying attention." She leaned closer to the screen and squinted. "You've spent over two hours listening to someone blab about the weather. It's raining. I figured that out all by myself."

Vince looked up at the ceiling with the intention of counting to ten. He made it all the way to four.

"Dammit, Katha, quit staring at that junk and listen to me."

She jumped to her feet and spun around, her eyes flashing. "That junk, mister, is hiding information we need to stop the—the perpetrators from stealing money that people desperately need."

He raised both hands. "Okay, okay, calm down. I know what you're doing is important, but so is what I have to say."

"Say it then."

"The streets in this area of town are flooding. That's not just a rainstorm out there, it's the tail end of a hurricane that was expected to stay out at sea, then shifted directions. So far, the phone lines are down in this general area, and they're closing off streets because of the water. Everyone is being told not to leave their homes. We're not in any danger because Tander's yacht has survived storms much worse than this. But. . . ." He paused. ". . . we can't drive home."

Her eyes widened. "What?"

"We're staying put until the streets are reopened. I radioed a buddy of mine, and he's calling Jane to tell her that you're safe, but stranded. I knew you wouldn't want her or your father to worry."

"Oh."

She wrapped her hands around her elbows and stared up at the ceiling as though to see the fury of the storm with her own eyes. She looked at Vince again.

"Are my father and Jane all right? Oh, you wouldn't know that, would you? Well, I'm sure they're fine. The house is well constructed, and Jane knows where the flashlight and candles are if the electricity goes off. They're snug as bugs, aren't they? Sure. And we're fine because this yacht is as sturdy as a battleship. Right? And . . ."

"Hey," Vince said gently.

He crossed the room to her and cradled her face in his hands.

"You're getting upset, Katha, and there's no reason to be worried. Everything is under control." Except him, he added silently. He hadn't intended to touch her, or even get close to her. But she looked so frightened, so small and vulnerable, her beautiful eyes wide with distress. He loved her, and he couldn't turn his back on her and walk out of the room while she was so scared. "There's nothing to be upset about. Trust me."

It was too much, Katha thought, it really was. She

was trying so hard to be cool and aloof. But so many things had happened while they'd been on that yacht, and she didn't have room to put them all. And now the storm . . . and Vince was being so strong and comforting, making her feel safe and protected and . . . It was just too much.

Two tears slid down her cheeks.

Vince groaned. "Katha, don't cry. Please, don't cry."

"No, I won't," she said, as two more tears followed the first. "I'm not."

"Come here." He dropped his hands from her face and wrapped his arms around her, drawing her close. She encircled his waist with her own arms and rested her head on his chest, loving his strength, his warmth, his caring.

They stood there, not moving, each lost in thoughts of love they refused to put into words. Each holding fast to the one who had captured their heart for all time. Each feeling the pulsing heat of desire growing and churning within them.

"Oh, Vince," Katha said, as she fought against her tears.

He closed his eyes and tightened his hold on her, not wishing to let her go, wanting to tell her that she was safe because he would always be there for her. Wanting to tell her that he loved her.

But he didn't speak. He buried his face in her fragrant curls and inhaled deeply, as though to take the very essence of her into himself. He willed his rising passion to remain under his command.

"I'm sorry," she said, making no attempt to move away. "I'm being childish. Storms don't really frighten me. It's just that . . . I'm all right. I'm fine."

"Good." He didn't release her. "Okay."

Seconds ticked into minutes, and still they didn't move.

"We may have to spend the night here," he said finally. "I'll keep tabs on things by listening to the shortwave radio. The rocking motion of the yacht isn't making you sick, is it?"

"No. Do you really think we'll be here all night?"

"It's a definite possibility."

"This yacht . . . I don't know . . . It's like being in another world, separate and apart from what's real. And now with the storm, it's as though we've been lifted up and away. I'm tempted to say, 'I have a feeling we're not in Kansas anymore, Toto.' "

He chuckled, but a moment later he was serious again.

"You're right," he said quietly. "It does feel as though we're in a place beyond the real world. *Our* place, Katha, where nothing can intrude unless we let it. There's just the two of us. No one else, nothing else."

"Yes, that's what I mean."

"Does that bother you, frighten you?"

"No," she whispered. How foolish this was, she thought. The harsh reality of truth was out there, waiting for her. But she didn't care, not now, because she was held safely in Vince Santini's arms. "No, I'm not frightened."

"In this place, our world, Katha, we can fly with the angels."

What in the hell was he saying? he asked himself. He should move her away from him, walk out of that room, keep as much distance between them as possible. But he wasn't going to, and at that moment he didn't give a damn that this was wrong, totally wrong. For now, Katha was in his arms where she belonged, and he wasn't going to let her go. Not yet.

She lifted her head, and their gazes met.

"Kiss me, Vince, please," she said.

He lowered his head and claimed her mouth, his tongue gaining entry, seeking hers. They drank of each other's sweet taste and their passions soared, matching the storm's fury. Hearts raced and breathing roughened as the kiss intensified, deepened to a hungry urgency. The embers of desire within them burst into leaping flames of want and need.

Vince slid his hands beneath Katha's sweater, then up to cup her aching breasts. His arousal was full, straining against the front of his jeans.

Never, he thought, would he get enough of her. To make love with Katha was like nothing he'd experienced before. She filled the void within him, warmed away his loneliness. There, in their private world, she was his. There, he didn't have to let her go.

"Make love with me, Vince," she whispered. "This is our place, our world. I want you."

With unsteady hands, he drew her sweater up and away, then dropped it onto the floor. Her bra followed close behind. He nestled her breasts in his hands, then leaned down to draw one rosy bud into his mouth. Katha clung to his upper arms, her head tipped back as she closed her eyes in ecstasy.

As Vince laved her breast with his tongue, then suckled, pulling the soft bounty deep into his mouth, his hands moved to the snap of her jeans. He unzipped the jeans, then dropped to one knee as he inched them down, catching her panties with his thumbs. As her dewy, flushed skin came into his view, he kissed her, nibbling, drawing lazy circles with the tip of his tongue.

Katha stepped free of her clothes, her entire body trembling. She sank to her knees, unable to stand for another moment, and reached for Vince's sweater. He raised his arms to allow her to remove it, then shuddered as she leaned forward to place whispering kisses across his chest. As her tongue found a nipple, he moaned, his manhood surging with potent need.

He grasped her arms and carefully lowered her to lie on the thick carpet. As she watched, he stripped off the rest of his clothes, then dropped down beside her. He rested one leg over both of hers as he sought her mouth, her tongue. His hand teased her nipples, then slid over her, igniting fires wherever it touched. Heat pulsed insistently deep within Katha's body. Her hands, too, roamed over Vince's moist skin, caressing, fluttering here, there, and everywhere. His muscles flexed and trembled beneath her feathery foray, and his manhood throbbed against her.

"Oh, please," she gasped. "Vince, please."

The last thread of his control snapped, and he moved over her and into her. He filled her with one deep thrust, then began to love her with movements as wild as the storm. She wrapped her legs around his powerful thighs and matched his pounding rhythm, clinging to his shoulders, whispering his name.

As rapture filled them, they flew to meet the angels. Seconds apart they reached the height of the exquisite sensations, holding nothing back as their bodies gave and received love.

With his last ounce of energy, Vince rolled onto his back, taking Katha with him, their bodies still meshed. He held her tightly as they drifted slowly downward and returned to the here and now. She nestled her head on his shoulder and sighed in sated pleasure.

They lay still, not speaking, not wishing to break the misty, sensual spell hovering around them.

"Beautiful," Vince finally said.

"Oh, yes."

"We're definitely not in Kansas anymore, Toto."

She smiled. "No."

"Oh, Lord, Katha, I . . ."

"Shh. No. It was wonderful, Vince, and we both wanted it so very much. Don't say anything, okay?

It was ours, in our private world. That's all that matters now. Please?"

"All right." He paused. "Can you feel me? Inside of you? Lord, it's good, just so damn good."

"Yes."

They were silent for several minutes.

"Did you ever have a dog like Toto?" Katha asked.

"No. My grandfather was allergic to dogs and cats. I've always wanted an English sheepdog. A big, funny, clumsy sheepdog. I'd name him Oliver."

"Perfect. I want a Chow Chow because they look like teddy bears. I'm going to name him Chow-Lee-Chan."

Vince chuckled. "That's a terrible name."

"I know, but I love it." And she loved Vince Santini. Oh, dear heaven, how she loved him. "Am I too heavy?" She wiggled a bit.

"No, you're as light as a feather, but . . . Katha, don't squirm around like that."

"Why not? I'm just getting more comfortable." She wiggled again. "I don't want to move away, but you're a rather hard pillow."

"Well put," he said, smiling. "That's the point I'm trying to make regarding why you'd better lie still."

"What . . . Oh," she gasped as she felt his manhood surge within her.

"Yes."

She wiggled.

He groaned.

Slowly, Katha eased upward to straddle his hips.

"Katha, are you sure you want . . ."

"Shh. Fly with me, Vincent. The angels are waiting for us."

And they flew.

Much later they showered together, then dressed. Katha made omelets, while Vince produced buttered toast, and they chatted while they ate, their conversation light and carefree.

"My father's birthday is coming up in a few days," Katha said after finishing her omelet.

"Does he have a favorite flavor of cake?" Vince asked, eyeing the remaining slice of toast.

"Nope. He likes cinnamon rolls for his birthday. You can have that toast. I'm stuffed."

Vince took the toast. "Cinnamon rolls for a birthday cake?"

"That's what he's had since I can remember. I'll make them from scratch, and put the birthday candles right in the middle of the welfare rolls." She blinked. "I mean the cinnamon rolls. That was my conscience speaking, telling me I'd better get back to work on the computer."

Vince chuckled, then frowned when he saw Katha stiffen in her chair, her eyes wide.

"Katha? What is it? What's wrong?"

"Oh, my gosh. Oh, good grief. Oh, Vince." She lunged to her feet.

He stood, too, his frown deepening. "Katha?"

"Vincent, did you hear what I said? Welfare rolls, cinnamon rolls. I've been through the program over and over, the one that prints the envelopes to mail the checks, and I swear the virus isn't there. What if I'm looking at the wrong program? Vince, what if the perpetrators aren't after the checks at all? What if they want the food vouchers for milk, cheese, cinnamon rolls, that stuff."

"Katha, that's crazy."

"Is it?" She ran from the room.

"Hey." He spun around. "Katha," he yelled after her, "high-tech criminals don't steal cinnamon rolls!"

Nine

Yes, they did.

After a teeth-clenching, floor-pacing hour, Vince whirled as Katha let out a shriek.

"I've got it! I've found it!" She stood and flung her arms around Vince's neck, smiling up at him. "We did it, Vince. The virus is there as clear as day."

He dropped a quick kiss on her lips. "*You* did it, Ms. Computer Genius. I'm very impressed."

"Don't be," she said, reluctantly drawing her arms away from his neck. "It's a very simple virus, and no attempt was made to layer it under other symbols, or disguise it in any way. The weird thing about it is that it instructs the computer to readdress a specific group of envelopes, not all of them. The virus only shows up on lines in the program for one bakery surplus store."

"Only one?" He frowned. "And only bakery products?"

She sat back down in front of the computer. "There," she said, placing a fingertip on the green screen. "See that? Those five symbols give instructions to erase the address after them. According to the message that came over my modem, a new address will be placed there before the first of the month, which is next week. The vouchers for the bakery products for that one outlet will be rerouted."

Vince nodded. "You're right, it's weird. Where's the store that's been targeted?"

"Here. Look. That's the address of the outlet, but I don't know where it is in the city."

"I do. It's down in the warehouse district."

Her head snapped up, and she looked at Vince. "The phone call we traced came from that area."

"Yep."

Vince began to pace the floor again, his eyes narrowed in concentration. Katha watched him trek back and forth. Thunder continued to rumble in the distance, and the rain beat against the windows. Vince finally stopped, staring over Katha's shoulder at the computer screen. He straightened and crossed his arms over his chest.

"Interesting," he said, "and very strange. Why would they go to all this trouble, then only hit one store? And why only bakery products?"

"They have a thing for whole wheat bread?" she said, then giggled. Vince glared at her. "Sorry. What do we do next? Are you going to take this information to the police, turn the whole deal over to them?" Oh, not yet, please, she thought. If he did that, their part in this would be finished, and Vince would walk out of her life forever. "Well?"

"No," he said slowly, "I don't think so."

Hooray! she cheered mentally. "Why not?"

Good question, Vince thought dryly. He could present this address to a buddy of his on the force in a neat little package with a big red bow. All the cops had to do was stake out the store and pick up the bun thieves when they arrived.

So, why wasn't he going to do it that way? Because . . . because, dammit, then his and Katha's roles in this would be over. He'd have to leave her, say that last good-bye, and he wasn't ready to do that. Not yet.

"Well . . . think about it, Katha," he said. "I'd feel like a jerk going to the cops with this. Vincent Santini, Private Investigator, has cracked a big one, boys. These scums are going to rip off a bunch of hamburger buns." Not bad, Santini, he thought. That sounded halfway reasonable. "They'd laugh from here to Sunday."

"Oh."

"I'm not saying that these jokers should get away with this, you understand. Messing with the city computer, breaking into the welfare rolls program, isn't small-time crime. It's what they're going after that makes it ridiculous. No, I think the best way to handle this is to see it through to the end."

"What do you mean?"

"We'll watch the program for when the new addresses are slipped in there, then I'll nab them when they show up at the bakery outlet with the vouchers. When I go to the cops, I'll have the crumbs with me, collared and cuffed."

Katha jumped to her feet. "Hold it, sir. I'm hearing an excess of the singular. *We* will stake out the bakery outlet. *We* will see this through to the end."

"Not a chance. They may just be ripping off bread for heaven only knows what reason, but they've gone to a lot of trouble to do it. I don't imagine they'll take kindly to being tripped up at the last minute. Things could get rough, Katha, and I don't want you involved."

"That's not fair, Vince. I was in on this from the beginning, and I've earned the right to be there. I won't get in your way, I promise. I'll be as quiet as a mouse in the corner. You can cuff and collar, or however that goes, but I want to be there when it happens."

He looked at her for a long moment, and she met his gaze directly, her chin lifted with determination, her lips pursed.

"All right, you win," he said. "It's against my better judgment, but you win. I want your word that you'll do as I say when this thing goes down. I couldn't handle it if you got hurt. I'll call the shots, and you do exactly what I tell you."

Katha smiled. "Okay, Lieutenant. Do you want me to salute, or click my heels together, or something?"

He chuckled and pulled her into his arms. "That won't be necessary, Miss Logan. We'll seal our deal this way."

His mouth melted over hers, and Katha returned the passionate kiss with total abandon, feeling the licking flames of desire race through her once again.

"Deal?" he asked, his breathing rough when he lifted his head.

"Deal."

In unspoken agreement, Vince led her from the room, and down the corridor to the bedroom. Through the hours of the night they made love, time and again. They slept, only to wake and reach for each other, their passion never fully quelled, the want and need never ending. In their private world, their private place, they flew with the angels over and over.

The following days seemed to Katha to be encased in a rosy glow of ecstasy. The storm blew out its fury, Jane and her father welcomed her home with more of their maddening, knowing smiles, and she and Vince fell into, in Katha's opinion, a deliciously scheduled pattern.

He arrived at the house in the late afternoon, and

hey went to Tander's yacht to check the computer
rogram. Tander had called from Alaska, Vince said,
nd was still tied up there straightening out the
ness involving his oil wells.

"I wonder why he never told me he owned oil
vells?" he said musingly, more than once. "He's
usually hot to go on and on about what pies he has
his fingers in."

"Beats me," Katha would say, shrugging.

They were magical days and lovemaking nights.
Vince took Katha home around midnight, and only
hen, as she lay alone in her own bed, did reality
ttempt to raise its ugly head. She refused to listen
o the taunting whispers in her mind, refused to
dmit that what she was doing would make the final
arting between her and Vince even more painful.

She'd pay the piper later, she'd decided as she
drifted off to sleep, a smile on her lips.

On the last day of the month, a week after Katha
discovered the virus in the computer program, she
ounched in the commands to bring the program
nto view on the green screen.

"Oh . . . my . . . goodness," she exclaimed softly.

"What is it?" Vince asked.

"They did it. Oh, my God, they did it. Look, Vince,
hose are new addresses for the envelopes that will
hold the vouchers for the outlet in the warehouse
district. I've memorized the others because I've seen
hem so often. The old ones are erased, the new
ones are in place."

"Bingo. The checks and vouchers go out tomor row, the first. They bring in temporary help once a month to stuff the envelopes. The computer prints in exact order, the vouchers arrive from the surplus distribution center in exact order, and the envelopes are filled by rote. Those people have no reason to question a thing. They do their job and go home. Well, this is it. They're mailed tomorrow, should arrive at their destination the next day, or the day after, at the latest."

"Vince, the vouchers for that store are going to three different addresses. There are three of them in on this. Don't you think you should have some help?"

"Tander is due back tonight. He can go with us. He called me at home early this morning."

"What time tonight do you expect him?"

"Late, very late. Come here, my Katha."

"Yes, sir, Lieutenant."

Early the next afternoon, Vince sat in a padded lounge chair on the deck of Tander's yacht, watch ing Tander dissolve in a loud, long fit of laughter.

"Bread, cookies, cinnamon rolls," Tander said, gasping for breath. "Oh, I love it, I love it. I've heard of stealing dough, but this takes the cake. What a great pun. Santini, you've made my day."

"Are you finished, Mr. Ellis?" Vincent asked blandly. "Or would you like another twenty minutes to come totally unglued?"

"I'll shut up," Tander said, grinning at him, "be-cause you're obviously getting ticked off. But you have to admit, Vince, this is one for the books. I'll control myself and not dump the 'I told you so' rou-tine on you."

"Big of you. I've talked to the manager of the sur-plus store and he's cooperating. We'll use his back room to watch the comings and goings. Do you want in on this, or not?"

"Hey, of course I want in. I wouldn't miss this for the world. You and I can handle three guys, no sweat. I'm surprised you're letting Katha get that close to the action, though."

"She'll stay out of the way. She says she has a right to be there, and she's got a valid point. She promised to follow my orders to the letter. Lord, if anything happened to her I . . ."

Tander's smile faded. "Vince, truth time. What about you and Katha? What are you feeling for her? She's a special lady and—"

"I love her," Vince said. He blinked, stunned by his outburst.

"That's how I read it early on," Tander said qui-etly. "I just wondered if you'd figured it out yet. Have you told her how you feel about her?"

Vince took a deep breath and let it out slowly. "No. No, and I don't intend to."

Tander leaned forward to rest his elbows on his knees, his fingers loosely laced together. "Why the hell not?"

"What purpose would it serve? 'I love you, Katha. See ya.' That stinks. I won't be seeing her again after we wrap up this welfare affair."

"Your mind has checked out and left the baggage, buddy. You're nuts."

"I'm very aware of what I'm doing, Tander. My views on marriage and detective work haven't changed. They don't mix, they don't match, end of story."

Tander sat back and looked at Vince for a long moment before speaking.

"You're right," he said. "You should bail out of this thing you have going with Katha as quickly as possible."

"I know."

"Because you don't deserve her."

Vince stiffened. "What?"

"You don't deserve Katha Logan. You've tossed her on the pile with a bunch of statistics that say cops have a high divorce rate. Never mind that she's been right in there pitching on this welfare number from the beginning, being your partner in helping to solve a crime. Sure enough, Santini, she's too fragile to live with a private investigator, to love him. She couldn't handle it." He shook his head. "You're so full of bull, Santini."

Vince pushed himself to his feet. "That's enough, Ellis. You're a real piece of work, do you know that? You talk because you like the sound of your own voice, ignoring the fact that you have no idea what you're talking about."

"Don't I, Vince?" Tander stood and met Vince's angry glare. "You've used that poor, tired excuse of yours to avoid a serious relationship, a commitment to a woman, ever since I've known you. And this time, chum, you're going to let the best thing that ever happened to you slip through your fingers."

"Now, look, Tander—"

"Forget it. I'm not interested in hearing any more of your crap. Get off my yacht, Santini, and let me get some sleep. I'm wiped out from tromping through the snow in Alaska. I'll see you tomorrow." He moved around Vince, then halted, looking at him over his shoulder. "Oh and, Vince? Did you ever stop to think about what it is you're really afraid of?"

Vince took one long step toward him, and his hand snapped out to close around Tander's muscular upper arm. "You're pushing me too far this time, Tander," he said through clenched teeth. "For two cents I'd—"

"Deck me?" Tander interrupted. "Go ahead, if it'll make you feel better. But even if you break my face, the facts aren't going to change."

Vince swore in Italian and released Tander's arm. He dragged a hand through his hair, then shook his head. "My mind is a mess."

"I know," Tander said, his voice gentling. "I know. You look like misery warmed over. Think about what I said, okay? You're going to lose Katha if you don't get your act together. I'm going to bed." He turned again and left the deck.

"See ya," Vince said quietly, then slowly walked across the yacht to the dock.

Tander stood in the shadows of the doorway and watched Vince leave. Think, Santini, he told him silently. For God's sake, think. He patted one cheek, then the other. "Handsome, knock-'em-dead face," he said aloud, "you nearly got yourself creamed." He grinned. "Ah, what grand work I do. Cupid, you owe me one, you lazy bum."

Vince drove away from the marina, his knuckles white from his tight hold on the steering wheel. Tander's words echoed maddeningly in his mind.

Did you ever stop to think about what it is you're really afraid of?

"Dammit," he said. Tander was crazy, totally nuts.

He glanced at his watch and pressed harder on the gas pedal. He had to meet the decorator at his new office, he suddenly remembered. He knew what kind of atmosphere he wanted to create, so it was just a matter of getting advice on how to put it all together. Then later he'd see Katha and . . .

Vince cursed again, and his scowl deepened. He *wasn't* seeing Katha that night because she was attending a Women in Business meeting. That was fine, he decided. He could use a peaceful evening at home, alone, without Katha filling the room with her bubbly laughter and cheerful chatter. No problem. He'd read a book, or watch television, or . . .

Did you ever stop to think about what it is you're really afraid of?

"Hell."

Early the next morning, Katha, Vince, and Tander, stood in the back room of the bakery surplus outlet.

"You know the setup," Vince said to them. "People can come in here off the street and pay cash for this stuff. The manager has the products to be redeemed by the welfare vouchers in a special place. When someone gives him a voucher today, he'll say, 'Do you think we'll get more rain?' That's our signal to move in, Tander. Katha, you stay put. Understand?"

"Got it," Tander said.

"Yes, I understand," Katha said quietly. Vince had hardly spoken to her since he'd picked her up. Maybe this was how he acted when he was in his detective mode, but he hadn't kissed her or even smiled at her. "I won't get in the way."

"Good." Lord, she was beautiful, he thought. What her green sweater did for those gorgeous eyes of hers was incredible. He wanted to haul her into his arms and kiss her until they couldn't breathe. He'd spent a lousy evening at home alone, and a restless night in his big empty bed. And Tander's insane question hadn't given him a moment's peace. Maybe he'd deck mouthy Mr. Ellis after all. "I'll take first watch. You two get comfortable."

He moved to the door, opened it a crack, then leaned one shoulder against the wall. His arms crossed over his chest, he frowned as he looked through the narrow opening.

"Gin rummy?" Tander asked Katha, taking a deck of cards from his shirt pocket. "A million dollars a point."

Katha pulled her gaze from Vince to look at Tander. "Pardon me? I'm sorry, I didn't hear what you said."

Tander smiled at her. "There's a lot of that going around. Come on, let's play cards."

Time ticked slowly by.

No one came into the store with welfare vouchers.

At noon, Tander slipped out the back door and returned with sandwiches and soft drinks.

"Eat and deal," he said to Katha. "I owe you fifty-seven million dollars. You're tapping out my petty cash."

"Shh," Vince said, eating his sandwich from his vantage point by the door. "Keep your voice down."

"You've got it, Mr. Sunshine," Tander said. "Want to play strip poker, Katha?"

"Hey!" Vince exclaimed.

"Mr. Santini, please," Tander said in mock indignation. "Keep your voice down. Do you want to blow this caper?"

Vince mumbled something that Katha decided

she was better off not hearing, and she dealt the cards.

Time continued to tick slowly by.

Vince refused Tander's offer to take a turn standing by the door.

A dark curtain of gloom settled over Katha.

At four-twelve in the afternoon, Vince stiffened and pushed away from the wall. His eyes narrowed as he peered through the opening of the door.

"Holy hell," he whispered.

Katha and Tander got to their feet.

"What—" Tander started.

Vince raised one hand to silence him, then motioned to them to come to the door.

The manager's voice rang out. "Do you think we'll get more rain?"

Tander reached for the gun at the back of his belt, then frowned in confusion as Vince shook his head. Vince took Katha's hand and moved her in front of him so she could see through the opening. Her eyes widened in shock, and her mouth formed a silent, astonished 'Oh'. Vince placed his hands on her shoulders and gently shifted her out of the way. Jerking his head at Tander, he opened the door and walked into the front of the store.

"Good afternoon, ladies," he said. "Hello, Martha Turnbull. How's that classic Studebaker of yours running? Fit as a fiddle?"

Martha gasped, one hand flying to her throat. The

purple tulip on her red hat bounced violently. The two elderly women with her stared at Vince with wide eyes, fear etched on their pale, wrinkled faces.

"Oh, blast," Martha said. "The jig is up. That's Vincent Santini, the detective, girls. He's a mean, tough cop. He doesn't mess around, just kicks tail and takes names. We're headed for the slammer."

"Kicks tail and—" Tander burst into laughter.

"Oh, hello, Katha dear," Martha said, smiling brightly as Katha inched her way into the room. "Your young man is about to haul me and the girls to the pokey."

"Martha," Katha said, "what on earth is this all about?"

"I want a lawyer!" one of the women yelled.

"Hush, Gladys," Martha said. "You can't afford a lawyer."

"I want one anyway," Gladys said. "A cute, young public defender will do. Male, of course."

"Enough of that," Katha said sternly. "Martha, you have some explaining to do. Did you break into the welfare department's computer program?"

"I certainly did," Martha said, puffing up with pride. "There's a computer and modem at the adult center where we go for our free hot lunch. I'm a computer whiz, I'll have you know. Mary Margaret . . . Say hello, Mary Margaret."

"Hello," Mary Margaret said in a shaky voice. "It's ever so nice to meet all of you."

"Mary Margaret," Martha went on, "lives across town, and there's a computer in her adult center too. We sent messages back and forth on the modems." She frowned at Mary Margaret. "Not that she answered me half the time."

"That's because some of your messages came over *my* modem," Katha said.

"Well, do tell." Martha clicked her tongue. "Silly me. My memory just isn't what it used to be. I must have dialed into your modem by mistake, confused your number with Mary Margaret's. Oh, old age is the pits. Thank heavens I had Peter to help—" She stopped abruptly.

"Peter?" Katha said. "Your grandson is involved in all of this?"

Martha shot Vince a worried glance. "Not exactly, dear. I mean, I do know my way around a computer. I started learning how to use them several years ago when Peter got so interested in them. And I am good with them, but not like Peter. You know he's getting a master's in computer science, Katha."

"I know. But what does he have to do with your breaking into the welfare department computers?"

"Oh, he gave us just a little bit of help. Not that he wanted to, mind you. Grandmothers do know how to use just the right pressure on their grandchildren." She looked Vince squarely in the eye. "So don't you go thinking you can press charges against Peter. He did everything completely against his will.

Gladys, Mary Margaret, and I take full responsibility for what we did. Don't we, ladies?"

"Absolutely," Gladys said. "Most fun I've had since we put that personals ad in the paper."

"But why?" Vince asked. "That's the question here. Why did you go to all that trouble to rip off bakery surplus from this particular store?"

"Gladys and I," Martha said, "live in public housing near here. Mary Margaret lives in public housing across town. We're all widows on fixed incomes, and simply didn't have the funds to purchase what we needed. Now, don't misunderstand, young man. We've already mailed the vouchers we didn't need back to the welfare department so the proper people can claim their goods. We only came here for . . ."

"For?" Katha, Vince, and Tander said in unison.

"Cinnamon rolls," Martha said, with a big smile. "Cinnamon rolls to celebrate Bobby's birthday. Oh, we could have pooled our pennies together and bought him a box of them at the supermarket, but those aren't nearly as good as bakery-made ones, and Bobby deserves the best. And not just one or two, but dozens of them. You could freeze them, Katha, and then he could celebrate his birthday for months. But . . ." she sighed. "You've caught us, so poor Bobby won't have any."

"Martha!" Katha exclaimed. "You did this for my father. You all did this to give my dad a birthday party."

Vince rubbed one hand across his forehead. "Oh, hell."

"I love it," Tander said, laughing. "What a scam. It's the crime of the century. The Over the Hill Gang strikes in force."

"We are not," Gladys said indignantly, "over the hill. We may be teetering on the top of the hill, but we're certainly not *over* it. Mind your manners, young man."

"I'm sorry, ma'am," Tander said. "I didn't mean to offend you."

"I should hope not. All you young people are alike. You think that once a person hits sixty-five, he might as well be dead. Well, Martha, Mary Margaret, and I are not about to be shuffled off to some nursing home where we can vegetate. Why, look what we've done, getting these vouchers. Who says you can't teach an old dog new tricks? Right, Martha?"

"Damn straight," Martha said. She fixed Katha, Vince, and Tander with a fierce look. "I bet it'll be a long time before any of you say a person's life is over at sixty-five."

They all nodded obediently, then Vince abruptly shook his head.

"Now hold it!" he said. "Just hold it here. Martha, I agree that we often don't give older people enough credit for what they're capable of, but do you have any idea what you've done? You've committed a crime, a third-degree felony. You're guilty of harmful access to a computer, which could get you a sentence of up to ten years in prison and a five-thousand-dollar fine."

"Do you," Martha said, her voice quivering slightly, "have any idea what it's like to live on the pittance we receive each month? To worry constantly that an unexpected expense will occur? To have to resort to accepting free meals at an adult center? To have a friend who is as dear to us as Bobby Logan is, and not have the money to give him a cinnamon roll birthday cake on his special day?"

"Oh, Martha," Katha said, tears in her eyes, "your hearts were in the right place, but Vince is right. What you did was very wrong."

Martha sighed. "I realize that now, dear." She held out her hands. "Handcuff us, Mr. Santini, and take us to the hoosegow."

The manager of the store dabbed at his eyes with a handkerchief, then blew his nose. "I didn't see or hear a thing. I won't testify against them."

"Vince?" Katha said, looking up at him. "What are you going to do with them?"

"He's going to toss 'em in the clink," Tander said. "He's a hard-core cop, you know."

"I want a cute lawyer!" Gladys cried.

"Everybody shut up!" Vince bellowed.

The entire populace of the store shut up.

"Thank you," Vince said.

He rubbed one hand slowly across his chin as he

stared at the three felons. The silence in the room was deafening.

"Martha Turnbull," he finally said, "do I have your solemn word that you'll never, ever, do anything like this again?"

"Oh, yes, dear. I really don't think I'm cut out for a life of crime, what with my silly lack of memory gumming up the works."

"Fine." Vince picked the vouchers up off the counter. "I'll see that these get back to the welfare department, and tell the supervisor that the program needs to be corrected. In the meantime . . ."

All eyes were riveted on Vince. He dug into his pocket and took out several bills, placing the money on the counter.

". . . buy Bobby Logan enough cinnamon rolls to make the biggest birthday cake he's ever seen."

Katha felt as though her heart would burst with love for Vincent Santini. "Thank you, Vince," she whispered.

"My bet was on you, Santini," Tander said. "I knew you'd come through. Now I'm heading home. Ladies, it was very refreshing to meet you."

"See ya, Tander," Vince said.

"Good-bye, Tander," Katha called, as he went out the front door.

Tander poked his head back into the store. "By the way, Vince, I don't own any oil wells in Alaska," he said, and disappeared.

Vince frowned for a moment, then turned to the

store manager. "Give the ladies what they want. Come on, Katha, let's get out of here."

As Vince and Katha came around the counter, Martha stepped in front of Vince, stood on tiptoe, and kissed him on the cheek, the purple tulip banging him on the forehead.

"Bless you, dear boy," she said softly. "Katha has chosen well."

Vince attempted a smile that didn't quite materialize, then lightly gripped Katha's elbow and led her from the store.

Lost in their own thoughts, neither spoke during the drive to Katha's house.

Ten

Vince parked the car in front of Katha's house, turned off the ignition, then crossed his arms on top of the steering wheel as he stared out the windshield.

Katha looked at him, not knowing if she should get out of the car, say something, or wait for him to speak.

"I imagine the gruesome threesome will be along soon," he finally said, "to have your father's birthday party."

"They meant well, Vince. What you did for them was wonderful."

"Right," he said, a sarcastic edge to his voice, "that's me, Mr. Wonderful." He sat back, shifting to face her. "The case is closed. Your crime has been solved."

And this was good-bye, Katha thought miserably. She'd known it was coming, but she hated it. She really hated it. She had to get through the next few minutes with dignity, with her pride intact. Somehow.

"Yes, it's—it's all over, isn't it?" she said softly, meeting his gaze. "I understand that."

Katha, Vince realized, wasn't talking about the ever-famous crime she'd discovered that had caused her to seek him out. She was referring to them, to what they'd shared. It was over. And it had to be this way.

Did you ever stop to think about what it is you're really afraid of?

Damn that Tander, Vince fumed. He didn't know what he was talking about. It was a ridiculous question, and he was ignoring it. Or he would, if Tander's words would get out of his brain and leave him in peace. Dammit, he had no room in his life for Katha Logan, for hearth and home, babies and puppies and PTA meetings. That's the way it was. That's the way it would always be.

"Katha, look, this time we've had together has been very . . . nice." Nice! Good Lord, had he actually said that god-awful word? It had been fantastic, beautiful beyond belief, flying with the angels to a place he hadn't even known existed. "I . . ."

She raised one hand. "Vince, please, a lengthy explanation isn't necessary." Her voice was steady. Wasn't it? He couldn't see the tears brimming in her eyes. Could he? She'd exit stage left with class.

Wouldn't she? "I know your stand on meshing the career of a private investigator with a commitment to one woman. I knew it from the beginning because you've been very honest about it."

She swallowed heavily and blinked back the threatening tears.

"I just want you to know," she added, her voice beginning to tremble, "that if I was given the chance to turn back the clock and rethink my decisions, I wouldn't do anything differently, even knowing it would end like this. What we shared was special, rare, and wonderful. I'll never forget you, Vince, but I understand why you have to go."

"But . . ."

She reached for the handle on the door, turning her head to hide her tears. "Thank you, Vince, for . . . Well, just thank you. I hope you'll be very happy and successful in your new career. Remember that when things pile up on you, and it's all heavy . . . remember to . . ." A sob caught in her throat. ". . . to fly with the angels." She opened the car door. "Good-bye."

"Katha, wait a minute."

She turned to look at him, tears streaming down her pale cheeks. "I didn't mean to cry. I promised myself I wouldn't cry. I've blown my Logan pride to smithereens. So"—she drew in an unsteady, tear-filled breath—"so I might as well go for the gusto. Vince, I just want you to know how much this all meant to me, what we had, what we shared. I—I love you, Vince. You're a warm, caring, beautiful man, and I'm so glad you touched my life. I do love you." She slid off the seat and ran up the front walk, disappearing into the house.

"Katha!" Vince yelled. He leaned across the seat of the car. "Katha! Come back here. I want to tell you . . . Hell."

He pulled the door closed with a resounding thud. After twisting the key in the ignition, he roared away from the curb.

Tell her what? his mind taunted him. That *he* loved *her*? No. He couldn't do that because saying the words wouldn't change a thing. Katha loved him? Lovely, precious, one-of-a-kind Katha was in love with him? It didn't matter, because he couldn't have her. He was a private investigator, alone. And Katha was all woman when he took her into his arms . . .

"Dammit, Santini, quit it," he muttered. "It's over. That's the way it has to be."

Did you ever stop to think about what it is you're really afraid of?

Vince groaned. "Ellis, I'm going to flatten you."

Through the hours of the night, the question hammered at Vince with no mercy. He sat in a chair in his living room, not bothering to turn on the lights, and stared at nothing. He sat and he thought, not moving until dawn's light announced the beginning of a new day.

And through the hours of that night, Katha cried.

She'd drawn on her last ounce of control and had taken part in the birthday party for her father with Martha and her cronies. She hadn't fooled her beloved father, she knew, and saw but ignored the worried looks he gave her. As soon as she could make her escape, she had fled to her room.

At dawn she dried her eyes, squared her shoulders, and lifted her chin.

Okay, she thought, she'd wept, as any woman of wisdom would do under the circumstances, knowing the healing powers of tears allowed to flow freely. She'd cried, and now she'd stop and move forward with her life. Without Vince.

And what about the pain in her aching heart? she asked herself. What about her shattered pride?

She frowned and shook her head. No, darn it, she hadn't destroyed her pride by telling Vince of her love for him. She'd spoken the truth, and she wasn't sorry. It had been the final words of a chapter in her life that she would cherish for all time. The memories were hers. Forever.

The days passed, and Katha threw herself into her work, putting in long hours of typing and proofing. When she fell into bed at night, she slept from pure exhaustion. But always hovering near in her mind's eye was the image of Vincent Santini.

A week after her final farewell to Vince, her father took her hand and held it tightly.

"Talk . . . to your . . . dad," he said. "Where . . . is Vince?"

"He's gone, Daddy," she said softly. "It's over between us."

"Do you . . . love . . . him?"

"Yes. Oh, yes, but I knew it would end. He never lied to me about that. He feels very strongly about his career not meshing with a serious relationship. I think he's wrong, but I respect his right to believe as he does. I'll be fine, in time. I just need a little more time."

"Maybe . . . flying . . . with the angels . . . would ease your . . . pain."

"No, Daddy, the angels can't help with this." She kissed him on the cheek. "I love you. Please don't worry about me." She smiled at him, then left the room.

Robert frowned and shook his head. "Foolish man . . . that Vince," he murmured. "And he . . . doesn't . . . know squat about . . . football teams . . . either."

On the day that marked the two-week anniversary of what Katha grimly referred to in her mind as the Big Good-bye, she dressed in dark blue slacks and a bright red-white-and-blue striped sweater.

She looked, she decided, peppy and cheerful, with

patriotic thrown in for good measure, and she was determined to keep the image of Vince at bay.

A knock sounded at the door as she crossed the living room, heading for her office, and she spun around to answer it. Smiling she flung open the door.

"Hello, Katha," Vince said.

Her smile disappeared as she blinked, then blinked again. Sure enough, Vince Santini was standing on her front porch. Big, strong, beautiful Vince, who looked exhausted, yet was still gorgeous in jeans and a caramel-colored sweater. Oh, good grief, why was Vince standing on her front porch?

"Why are you standing on my front porch?" she asked.

"Did you mean it? Do you love me, Katha?"

"Vince, please don't. There's no point in—"

"Did you mean it?" he repeated.

"Yes," she said with a sigh.

"Katha, would you go for a drive with me? Please?"

"Why?"

"It's important. I know I don't have the right to ask anything of you, but will you do this for me, please?"

Not on your life, buster, she thought. "Yes," she heard herself say. "Just let me tell Jane that I'm leaving to go . . . wherever it is we're going. This is absurd."

"No, it's important," he said again.

Within ten minutes after driving away from the Logan home, Katha realized an astonishing fact. Vince Santini was nervous. He didn't speak nor look at her, but drummed his fingers on the steering wheel and fiddled with the radio. The man was a nervous wreck.

The man, she admitted, was also causing her heart to race. The two weeks since she'd seen him had done nothing to diminish the flame of love and desire within her.

"Where are we going?" she asked at last.

He didn't look at her.

"Trust me."

"Mmm," she said, and crossed her arms, staring out the side window.

Vince drove several miles south of the city, then turned onto a winding road that sloped upward. It led, Katha knew, to an area where huge, expensive homes had been built on large plots of land above the city. Another ten minutes passed, then Vince slowed. He drove between two concrete pillars onto a curving driveway that ended at an enormous two story white house that gleamed in the sunshine.

"What a beautiful house," Katha exclaimed. "Whose car is that in front?"

"Tander's." Vince pulled in behind the sleek, silver Jaguar and turned off the ignition.

"Tander lives here?"

"No." Vince got out of the car.

Katha opened her door and scrambled out. "Then who lives here?" she asked.

"Trust me. Come on."

They went up the sweeping front steps, across the wide porch, then Vince opened the door and stepped back for Katha to proceed inside.

"You didn't knock," she said.

"Trust me."

"Your record's stuck," she said, then stomped into the house.

The house, she realized, coming to a dead stop, had no furniture. The enormous front foyer was tiled in pink marble, and the wood floors of the spacious rooms gleamed, but there wasn't any furniture.

A door halfway down the long hall opened and Tander emerged, closing the door behind him.

"Hi, sweetheart," he said, smiling at Katha as he walked toward them.

"Hello, Tander," she said, returning his smile.

"I'm gone, Vince. You'll get my bill. I charge thousands for baby-sitting."

"I owe you for more than that," Vince said, no trace of a smile on his face.

Tander opened the door and turned to look at Vince. "Don't blow it," he said seriously. "Just don't blow it." He left the house, and a few moments later the sound of a powerful engine being started filled the air, then faded into the distance.

"Baby-sitting?" Katha asked.

"Come into the living room," Vince said, and crossed the hall.

Katha stared after him for a moment, then slowly followed.

The living room had floor-to-ceiling windows on two sides, a flagstone fireplace, an exquisite oriental rug, and no furniture. Sunshine poured through the windows, shining on the white walls.

Vince shoved his hands into his pockets, pulled them free, folded his arms across his chest, then pushed his hands back into his pockets.

A nervous wreck, Katha thought again. "This is a beautiful rug," she said to break the silence.

"What?" He stared blankly at the rug. "Yes, it is. It was my grandfather's. It was one of the few things of his I kept when he died."

"Oh." His grandfather's rug? What was it doing here?

"Katha, I . . ." Vince started, then cleared his throat and tried again. "I left you two weeks ago believing I had no choice but to go. I'd convinced myself many years ago that my career didn't mix with a serious relationship."

"I know," she said quietly.

"Then you came into my life, filling what I realized was a cold, empty place inside me. What we shared was beautiful, very, very beautiful."

"Yes."

"But I still hung onto my vow that I'd never commit myself to one woman for all time. That was the way it was, had to be. Then Tander made me face a very difficult question. He asked me if I'd ever thought about what I was *really* afraid of."

"Afraid of? You explained that to me. You said the divorce rate in marriages where the man was a police officer was terribly high."

He shook his head. "That was the excuse I used for all those years to avoid commitment, to make certain I never loved. I used it for so long, I actually believed that was how I felt."

"I don't understand."

"I wouldn't have either, if it hadn't been for Tander and his question. Katha, I loved my parents and they were killed. They left me when I was a little boy. I loved my grandfather, but he had a wanderlust spirit, and every time I made friends he packed me up and moved me to another city, even another country. Then he grew old and died. He left me. I have a close friendship with Tander and a man named Declan Harris, but I've kept everyone else, men and women, at arm's length because—because I was afraid. To care, Katha, to love, was to be left alone . . . and lonely."

"Oh, Vince," she murmured.

"I've faced my ghosts, Katha. I've faced the truth about myself, that flaw, that fear. I faced it all, fought the battle, and won. It was the toughest fight of my life, but I had to win because if I lost, then I'd have lost you. My fears would have kept me from telling you how very much I . . . how very much I . . . Dammit, Katha, I love you!"

"You love me?" she repeated, her voice choked.

"I swear to God I love you," he said, his own voice husky with emotion. "Katha, I'm a cop, a private cop now, but still a cop, and always will be."

"Yes, of course, that's a part of who you are."

He nodded. "I'm a cop, but I'm also a man, a lonely man, who loves you and the warmth you bring into my life more than I can ever begin to tell you. I bought this house . . . for us, I hope. You can run your business from here if you want to. It's big enough for all of us . . . you, me, Jane, and your father. You're a package deal, I know that, because that's part of who *you* are. We'll be a family, all of us together, along with our children. Oh, Katha, please say you'll marry me. I don't want to be lonely anymore, and I do love you so damn much. Katha, please?"

She flung herself into his arms, clasping his neck. He held her tightly to him.

"Katha?"

"Yes! Yes, yes, yes." She tilted her head back to smile up at him through tears of happiness. "Yes, I'll marry you, have your babies, live in this wonderful house with you. Oh, Vince, I love you. I've missed you, ached for you, cried so much when I thought about you. Oh, my Vincent, you are my life."

Tears shimmered in both of their eyes. Vince lowered his head and kissed Katha gently, reverently.

Then the kiss deepened. It spoke of the pain and confusion of the past two weeks, of battles fought and won. It spoke of desire, growing with every beat of pounding hearts. It spoke of love. And commitment for all time.

"I love you, Katha Logan," Vince said, when he raised his head.

"And I love you, Vincent Santini," she whispered, then paused. "Vince, who was Tander baby-sitting?"

"Oh, Lord, I forgot about them."

"Them?"

He grabbed her hand and started across the room. Katha nearly had to run to keep up with him. Down the hall he opened the door to the room Tander had come out of, and led Katha inside.

"Oh!" she gasped.

In the center of what was obviously a library, sat a playpen. In the playpen was one fluffy white bundle and one tan, wiggling bundle.

"Ma'am," Vince said, with a sweep of his arm, "meet the rest of our family. One English sheepdog named Oliver, and one Chow Chow named Chow-Lee-Chan."

Katha laughed in delight, then ran forward to scoop the puppies up into her arms. They licked her face and wagged their tails.

"Welcome home, Mrs. Santini," Vince said.

"It's wonderful to be here, Mr. Santini," she said, smiling at him with love shining in her eyes.

They played with the puppies until the furry babies yawned and were more than ready to settle back down in the playpen for a nap.

Vince circled Katha's shoulders with his arm, and they returned to the living room.

Then there, on the oriental rug in the waterfall of sunshine, they made love.

There, in the house that would become their home that would overflow with love and laughter, Katha and Vince flew with the angels. . . .

THE EDITOR'S CORNER

As is the case with many of you, LOVESWEPT books have been a part of my life for a very long time—since before we ever published book #1, in fact. Having worked with Carolyn Nichols for over seven years, there's no way I could not have been caught up in her enthusiasm for and devotion to the LOVESWEPT project. I hope I can convey my excitement over the wonderful books we publish as entertainingly as Carolyn has over the years in the Editor's Corner.

Since next month is April, we're going to shower you with "keepers." Our six books for the month are sure to coax the sun from behind the clouds and brighten your rainy days.

Continuing her *Once Upon a Time* series, Kay Hooper brings you **WHAT DREAMS MAY COME,** LOVESWEPT #390. Can you imagine what Kelly Russell goes through when, a week before her wedding, her fiancé, John Mitchell, has a tragic accident which leaves him in a coma? Ten years later Kelly is finally putting the past behind her when Mitch arrives on her doorstep, determined to rekindle the love fate had stolen from them. Kay involves the reader from page one in this poignant, modern-day Rip Van Winkle story. Your emotions will run the gamut as you root for brave survivor Kelly and enigmatic Mitch to bridge the chasm of time and build a new life together.

Sandra Chastain has the remarkable ability to create vivid characters with winning personalities. Her people always lead interesting, purposeful lives—and the hero and heroine in **ADAM'S OUTLAW,** LOVESWEPT #391, are no exceptions. Toni Gresham leads a group of concerned citizens called Peachtree Vigilantes, who are out to corral muggers who prey on the elderly. Instead she swoops down from a tree with a Tarzan yell and lands atop police captain Adam Ware! Adam, who is conducting his own sting operation, is stunned to discover he's being held captive by an angel with golden curls. You'll laugh as the darling renegade tries to teach the lone-wolf lawman a thing or two about helping people—and in return learns a thing or two about love.

I suggest saving Janet Evanovich's **SMITTEN,** LOVESWEPT #392, for one of those rainy days this month. There's no way that after reading this gem of a romance you won't be smiling and floating on air! Single mom Lizabeth Kane wasn't exactly construction worker material, but she
(continued)

figured she could learn. The hours were good—she'd be home by the time her kids were out of school—and the location—the end of her block—was convenient. Matt Hallahan takes one look at her résumé—handwritten on spiral notebook paper—then at the lady herself, and he's instantly smitten. When the virile hunk agrees to hire her, Lizabeth's heart—and her libido—send up a cheer! Lizabeth never knew that painting a wall could be a sensual experience or that the smell of sawdust could be so enticing, but whenever Matt was near, he made her senses sizzle. Janet adds some zany secondary characters to this tender story who are guaranteed to make you laugh. For an uplifting experience, don't miss **SMITTEN!**

April showers occasionally leave behind rainbows. Tami Hoag brings you one rainbow this month and two more over the next several months in the form of her three-book series, *The Rainbow Chasers*. The Fearsome Foursome was what they called themselves, four college friends who bonded together and shared dreams of pursuing their hearts' desires in a sleepy coastal town in northern California. In **HEART OF GOLD,** LOVESWEPT #393, Tami picks up on the lives of the friends as one by one they realize their dreams and find the ends of their personal rainbows. Faith Kincaid is just about to open her inn and begin to forget her former life in Washington, D.C., when elegantly handsome Shane Callan—Dirty Harry in disguise—arrives on assignment to protect her—a government witness in a bribery trial. Faith has never known the intoxicating feeling of having a man want her until Shane pulls her to him on a darkened staircase and makes her yearn for the taste of his lips. Shane, lonely and haunted by demons, realizes Faith is his shot at sanctuary, his anchor in the storm. **HEART OF GOLD** is a richly textured story that you won't be able to put down. But Tami's next in the series won't be far behind! Look for **KEEPING COMPANY** in June and **REILLY'S RETURN** in August. You can spend the entire summer chasing rainbows!

Courtney Henke is one of the brightest new stars on the LOVESWEPT horizon. And for those of you who wrote after reading her first book, **CHAMELEON,** asking for Adam's story, Courtney has granted your wish—and delivered one sensational story in **JINX,** LOVESWEPT #394. How much

(continued)

more romantic can you get than a hero who falls in love with the heroine even before he meets her? It's Diana Machlen's ethereal image in an advertisement for the perfume her family developed that haunts Adam's dreams. But the lady in the flesh is just as tempting, when Adam—on a mission to retrieve from her the only written copy of the perfume formula—encounters the lovely Diana at her cabin in the Missouri Ozarks. Diana greets Adam less than enthusiastically. You see, strange things happen when she gets close to a man—and there's no way she can stay away from Adam! The chain of events is just too funny for words as Adam vows to prove her wrong about her jinx. Don't miss this delightful romp!

Deborah Smith's name has been popping up in more and more of your letters as one of the favorite LOVESWEPT authors. It's no wonder! Deborah has an imagination and creative ability that knows no bounds. In **LEGENDS,** LOVE-SWEPT #395, Deborah wisks you from a penthouse in Manhattan to a tiny village in Scotland. At a lavish party billionaire Douglas Kincaid can't help but follow the mysterious woman in emerald silk onto his terrace. Elgiva MacRoth wants the brutally handsome dealmaker—but only to kidnap him! She holds him captive in order to preserve her heritage and convince him to give up his land holdings in Scotland. But soon it's not clear who is the prisoner and who is the jailer as Douglas melts her resistance and revels in her sensuality. These two characters are so alive, they almost walk right off the pages. Deborah will have you believing in legends before you finish this mesmerizing story.

Look for our sparkling violet covers next month, and enjoy a month of great reading with LOVESWEPT!

Sincerely,

Susann Brailey

Susann Brailey
Editor
LOVESWEPT
Bantam Books
666 Fifth Avenue
New York, NY 10103

FAN OF THE MONTH

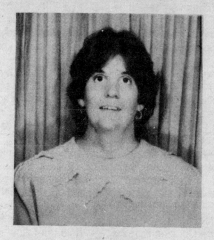

Kay Bendall

What a thrill and an honor to be selected a LOVE-SWEPT Fan of the Month! Reading is one of the joys of my life. Through books I enter worlds of enchantment, wonder, adventure, suspense, beauty, fantasy, humor, and, above all else, a place where love conquers all.

My favorite books are LOVESWEPTs. Each and every month I am impressed and delighted with the variety and excellence of the selections. I laugh, cry, am inspired, touched, and enjoy them all.

Kay Hooper, Joan Elliott Pickart, Iris Johansen, Deborah Smith, Barbara Boswell, and Peggy Webb are some of my favorite LOVESWEPT authors. The blend of familiar and new authors ensure that LOVESWEPTs will remain innovative and number one among the romance books.

The day the mailman brings my LOVESWEPTs is my favorite day of the month!

OFFICIAL RULES TO
LOVESWEPT'S
DREAM MAKER GIVEAWAY
(See entry card in center of this book)

1. NO PURCHASE NECESSARY. To enter both the sweepstakes and accept the risk-free trial offer, follow the directions published on the insert card in this book. Return your entry on the reply card provided. If you do not wish to take advantage of the risk-free trial offer, but wish to enter the sweepstakes, return the entry card only with the "FREE ENTRY" sticker attached, or send your name and address on a 3x5 card to : Loveswept Sweepstakes, Bantam Books, PO Box 985, Hicksville, NY 11802-9827.

2. To be eligible for the prizes offered, your entry must be received by September 17, 1990. We are not responsible for late, lost or misdirected mail. Winners will be selected on or about October 16, 1990 in a random drawing under the supervision of Marden Kane, Inc., an independent judging organization, and except for those prizes which will be awarded to the first 50 entrants, prizes will be awarded after that date. By entering this sweepstakes, each entrant accepts and agrees to be bound by these rules and the decision of the judges which shall be final and binding. This sweepstakes will be presented in conjunction with various book offers sponsored by Bantam Books under the following titles: Agatha Christie "Mystery Showcase", Louis L'Amour "Great American Getaway", Loveswept "Dreams Can Come True" and Loveswept "Dream Makers". Although the prize options and graphics of this Bantam Books sweepstakes will vary in each of these book offers, the value of each prize level will be approximately the same and prize winners will have the options of selecting any prize offered within the prize level won.

3. Prizes in the Loveswept "Dream Maker" sweepstakes: Grand Prize (1) 14 Day trip to either Hawaii, Europe or the Caribbean. Trip includes round trip air transportation from any major airport in the US and hotel accomodations (approximate retail value $6,000); Bonus Prize (1) $1,000 cash in addition to the trip; Second Prize (1) 27" Color TV (approximate retail value $900).

4. This sweepstakes is open to residents of the US, and Canada (excluding the province of Quebec), who are 18 years of age or older. Employees of Bantam Books, Bantam Doubleday Dell Publishing Group Inc., their affiliates and subsidiaries, Marden Kane Inc. and all other agencies and persons connected with conducting this sweepstakes and their immediate family members are not eligible to enter this sweepstakes. This offer is subject to all applicable laws and regulations and is void in the province of Quebec and wherever prohibited or restricted by law. In order to win a prize, residents of Canada will be required to correctly answer a time-limited arithmetical skill-testing question.

5. Winners will be notified by mail and will be required to execute an affidavit of eligibility and release which must be returned within 14 days of notification or an alternate winner will be selected. Prizes are not transferable. Trip prize must be taken within one year of notification and is subject to airline departure schedules and ticket and accommodation availability. Winner must have a valid passport. No substitution will be made for any prize except as offered. If a prize should be unavailable at sweepstakes end, sponsor reserves the right to substitute a prize of equal or greater value. Winners agree that the sponsor, its affiliates, and their agencies and employees shall not be liable for injury, loss or damage of any kind resulting from an entrant's participation in this offer or from the acceptance or use of the prizes awarded. Odds of winning are dependant upon the number of entries received. Taxes, if any, are the sole responsibility of the winners. Winner's entry and acceptance of any prize offered constitutes permission to use the winner's name, photograph or other likeness for purposes of advertising and promotion on behalf of Bantam Books and Bantam Doubleday Dell Publishing Group Inc. without additional compensation to the winner.

6. For a list of winners (available after 10/16/90), send a self addressed stamped envelope to Bantam Books Winners List, PO Box 704, Sayreville, NJ 08871.

7. The free gifts are available only to entrants who also agree to sample the Loveswept subscription program on the terms described. The sweepstakes prizes offered by affixing the "Free Entry" sticker to the Entry Form are available to all entrants, whether or not an entrant chooses to affix the "Free Books" sticker to the Entry Form.

THE DELANEY DYNASTY

Men and women whose loves an passions are so glorious
it takes many great romance novels by three bestselling
authors to tell their tempestuous stories.

THE SHAMROCK TRINITY

☐ 21975   RAFE, THE MAVERICK
             by Kay Hooper $2.95

☐ 21976   YORK, THE RENEGADE
             by Iris Johansen $2.95

☐ 21977   BURKE, THE KINGPIN
             by Fayrene Preston $2.95

THE DELANEYS OF KILLAROO

☐ 21872   ADELAIDE, THE ENCHANTRESS
             by Kay Hooper $2.75

☐ 21873   MATILDA, THE ADVENTURESS
             by Iris Johansen $2.75

☐ 21874   SYDNEY, THE TEMPTRESS
             by Fayrene Preston $2.75

THE DELANEYS: *The Untamed Years*

☐ 21899   GOLDEN FLAMES *by Kay Hooper* $3.50
☐ 21898   WILD SILVER *by Iris Johansen* $3.50
☐ 21897   COPPER FIRE *by Fayrene Preston* $3.50

Buy them at your local bookstore or use this page to order.

Bantam Books, Dept. SW7, 414 East Golf Road, Des Plaines, IL 60016

Please send me the items I have checked above. I am enclosing $_____
(please add $2.00 to cover postage and handling). Send check or money
order, no cash or C.O.D.s please.

Mr/Ms _____

Address _____

City/State _____ Zip _____

Please allow four to six weeks for delivery.   SW7—11/89
Prices and availability subject to change without notice.